P9-APH-664

STINK

Boys don't mind giving off a pungent human aroma or smelling one. *Especially* if it involves a little perspiration.

If you know a great deal about natural science—or if you watch dogs much, which amounts to the same thing—you know that males have been given the primary responsibility for emitting and savoring odor in nature.

But—well, we seem to kind of even *like* it.

BRUCE BROOKS

BOYS WILL BE

HYPERION PAPERBACKS FOR CHILDREN
NEW YORK

Text© 1993 by Bruce Brooks.
All rights reserved.
No part of this book may be used or reproduced
in any manner whatsoever without written
permission from the publisher.
Printed in the United States of America.
For information address Hyperion Books for Children,
114 Fifth Avenue, New York, NY 10011.
Originally published in hardcover
by Henry Holt and Company, Inc. in 1993.

SCHOOL BOOK FAIR EDITION

Brooks, Bruce.
Boys will be/Bruce Brooks—1st Hyperion paperback ed.
p. cm.
Originally published: New York: H. Holt. 1993.
ISBN 0-7868-1106-4
1. Boys—United States. [1. Boys.] I. Title.
[HQ775.B7 1995]
305.23—dc20   94–3599

For Alex and Spence

Contents

To Boys
3

Nonexclusionary Introduction
5

Chitchat
9

The Cap
17

Risky Pals
26

Bullies
40

Questions for the Gunners
54

Stink
56

Real Boys Read Books
62

**Ten Things
You Cannot Expect Your Mom
to Come Close to Understanding**
73

**Eight Reasons Why Ice Hockey
Kicks Football's Tutu**
76

Victory
102

Arthur Ashe
115

Respect
124

BOYS
WILL BE

To Boys

You will notice that some of these essays are written directly to you, while others seem to be addressing adults—vaguely directed at fathers, mothers, teachers, and so on. Sometimes within a single essay I jump from a point aimed at you to a point aimed at adults. Don't be put off. I do this on purpose, and I don't want you to feel you are being excluded when I don't seem to be talking right to you. This whole book is intended for *you* to read.

When I seem to be addressing your father or your teacher, well, then you are *invited* to spy on us. I see nothing wrong with selective eavesdropping; in fact, often in the middle of conversations in which adults are discussing boys, I say to myself, "I wish boys could hear this; I wish a hundred boys were hiding behind that sofa." But boys don't hear it, because we adults have a way of changing how we speak when we come right at you. Sometimes the change is nec-essary, but sometimes it isn't. We don't have to pretend as much as we think we do. We don't have to hide as much, either.

When you read these parts—when you eavesdrop—it may come as a surprise to you how seriously adults take a lot of your life, how much we think about your stuff. You can't always tell this from the way we present ourselves to you, because many of us don't speak up until something goes wrong, until correction, discipline, and punishment are called for. You can't always tell the discipline was preceded by a lot of analysis and understanding, but often it was.

So go ahead, feel comfortable spying. It's your book. And if you want to let your father, your mother, or your teacher spy on *you*—if there are things you think they could learn by eavesdropping on the parts of the book addressed to *you*—then pass the book around. Sometimes books are a good way to let people in on things they otherwise cannot bring themselves to see, by letting them read things we otherwise cannot bring ourselves to say.

Nonexclusionary Introduction

This is a book about boy stuff, written for boys to read, by a former boy who is now raising two boys of his own. So, naturally, I'd like to extend a very warm welcome to all the—*girls*! Hi, girls!

Legally speaking, I'm sure there is no such thing as "boy stuff." If I try even to imply that a girl's interest may be excluded from, say, the chapter on body odor resulting from athletics (you eager boys can turn there now: it's on page 56), it is very likely a federal judge can force me to write a precisely-equal-length book for girls. With articles about, oh, I don't know, the pros and cons of sparkle in lip gloss, or the twelve best ways of sucking up to teachers and making them think you are just the most devoted little helpful student in the whole wide world.

Joking! Only joking, Judge! But do you see my problem? I know girls are actually serious human beings, but when I reach for confirming details, I often find silly stereotypes instead. (Kind of like the ones most females find when they think about boys.) There have been periods of my life when I was fundamentally interested in girls, when I even more or less *studied* them with a profound need to understand the subtleties, but the fact is, I don't know enough. Perhaps if I had daughters, I would be better equipped. I do have a wife, and she is terrific, but I didn't get to know her until her girlhood was past. It's too late for her to clue me in on even something as basic as the appeal of, for example, Betsy Wetsy, the Doll Who Really Pees! I happen to know she possessed a Betsy Wetsy, but we never discuss such things. We tend more to talk about difficult adult subjects, such as, oh, whether it's better to do the dishes after the kids are in bed and you are tired or leave them until the morning when you are fresher but when, because of the daylight, you have less of an excuse for missing spots. Things like that. It's hard to isolate the uniquely female components of reasoning in such analytical discussions.

So, hey, girls, all I can say is—you are invited to read this book because, of course, it is as much for you as it is for any mere boy. And I'm sure I better add that, you know, it's *about* you, too. I mean, *you* sweat, right, when *you* play street hockey and then stink, don't you? Sure! And you kind of *like the smell* just as boys do (once again, that's page 56). And you wear baseball caps every minute of your life from age four to age twenty-six (page 17)—I see you wearin' those caps all over the place! And you get in fistfights with bullies (page 40), you want to know why ice hockey is better than football (page 76), nobody wants to see you reading (page 62), you are worried about other girls shooting you with guns in your school (page 54), and you want to win more than anything else (page 102). We can *all* share these major elements of contemporary inner life.

And, no doubt, you are ready to share the incredible burden of being regarded by everyone as the totally wicked source, for now and the foreseeable future, of nearly all the horrid social problems in the United States of America. Yes! Everyone knows it's boys, and the men they become, who have invented and promoted war, the drug culture, racial oppression, illiteracy, AIDS, semiautomatic weaponry, overpriced sneakers, crummy violent movies and TV shows, and industrial pollution. Everybody knows on any given day you can read in the newspaper about how wretched and gross we are, or hear lectures at fine universities about how wretched and gross we are, or read books of social criticism about how wretched and gross we are. *This* book, I hope, is a rare chance for boys to read about themselves without being cursed and slammed down. A chance, for a few pages, for boys to unfasten the load of society's self-righteous anger. If you want to share the pages, you are also welcome to share in the unfastening. Who knows, maybe we *are* all pretty equal.

Chitchat

ere we are, drinking a few chilled Yoo-Hoos with Jason LaAntoine Gonzales-Wong, an unbelievably typical eleven-year-old male, and we are about to ask him a serious question:

BOOK: Say, JL—who is better, boys or girls?

JL: You got to be kidding, man.

BOOK: No, believe it or not, there are people who differ on this matter, so just answer: Who do you like best? Who do you want to depend on? Who's the go-to, the hang-with, the be-like? Is it the boy-human or the girl-human?

JL: Girls are not human.

Thanks for sharing. We will take Jason LaAntoine's response as a vote for boys, and we will bet you get the same vote from every single eleven-

year-old male in the United States. One day, of
course, most of these inherently surly, politically
confused guys will discover and enjoy the bliss of an
egalitarian partnership with a gender-differentiated
social unit, but—during a certain age boys enjoy
the company only of boys. In fact, every boy would
prefer to talk to *any* boy, even the one who does
his math homework early and doesn't know if the
Bulls represent basketball or rodeo and reads during recess, even *him* rather than five seconds with
the most-nearly-okay girl in the school. This is the
nature of life.

So why, then, do boys usually speak to each other
as if they felt nothing but contempt, hatred, and fe-
rocity? Why do they treat other boys so badly?

Worse than they treat girls. Worse, *far* worse than
they treat dogs or hamsters or captured snakes. It
would simply never occur to a boy to walk up to a
box turtle sunning itself on a rock in the woods and
say, "Yo, Buttface! Did you know your eyes are
crossed and your nostrils look like a two-car ga-
rage?" Yet this is precisely the sort of comment a
normal-looking fifth grader will offer, almost off-
handedly, to a normal-looking third grader quietly
studying his baseball cards on a window seat in the
school bus. Boy *A* walks by and sees Boy *B*, whom
he doesn't know or dislike or anything, and without
even thinking, Boy *A* lightheartedly sneers and tosses
off a few nasty insults. No big deal.

Sometimes, it really isn't. Sometimes, Boy *B* will look up briefly with a bored air, then resume studying his cards without a ripple of discomfort. But sometimes, more often than we like to think and certainly more often than Boy *A* imagines possible, Boy *B* will bite his quivering lip, run home the second he gets off the bus, stare for three hours into the mirror at his nose and eyes, then spend the evening trying not to cry or stab himself in the heart with a pencil—because of the newly noted condition of his face, sure, but more, much more, because of the utterly surprising burst of wanton aggression from Boy *A*. And then Boy *B* will grow up to be a serial ax murderer, or someone who devises standardized multiple-choice aptitude tests, or another similar predatory avenger getting back at society.

Let's check in with JL.

BOOK: Yesterday you went up to Titus Dukmejian McMurdo on the playground and told him— we have it on tape—that he eats mule boogers in hot-dog rolls, cannot go to sleep without a pink fur bunny he calls Lollipop, and is going to die of leprosy, as can be plainly seen by the scaly condition behind his rotting ears. Then you grinned, gave a little wave, and skipped off to shoot baskets with four other boys. Is this accurate?

JL: I thought it was a yellow fur bunny. But okay.

BOOK: Let's talk about why you spoke in this manner
    to Titus.

JL [*looking slightly perplexed*]: What manner?

BOOK: An aggressive, hurtful, sneering, threatening
    manner. Do you hate Titus for some reason?

JL [*more perplexed*]: Hate him? No. He's an okay
    guy.

BOOK: Has he ever insulted you?

JL: Nope.

BOOK: Have you and Titus ever had any sort of
    encounter?

JL: Well . . . one time he gave me a piece of his ham-
    spread sandwich at lunch.

BOOK: I see. Was it good?

JL: Oh, yeah. Ham spread is cool.

And so it goes. Most of the time, a boy who insults
another boy won't have any sense of causal inspiration—he won't feel events have somehow entitled
him to trash the kid. So he won't have constructed
any defense, any rationale or justification for being
nasty. The very question of defense seems weird.
What's the *problem*? All I did was say . . .

If beauty is in the eyes of the beholder, is nastiness?
When JL says sincerely that he had no meanness in
his heart, no intention of crippling Titus's ego, but
was just kind of, you know, *talking*—then does this
mean he is just kind of, you know, innocent? Innocent, at least, of meanness? The words are still there,

burning Titus's ears. But the wanton aggression—is it perhaps imagined?

I hate to say it, but I think so. I hate to say it because I was always puzzled by the trash talk when I was growing up. If you called me something horrible, I definitely felt victimized and hurt, and I worried long and angrily about what you had against me. I also felt, quite strongly, that you should be put to death. To me, there was no excuse for such aggressive hurtfulness.

I was wrong. There is an excuse. Taunting is just a way of messing with language, seeing what it can do, *testing* it, in its most extreme form, to see if it has any power. And then of using this powerless thing with an entirely careless attitude.

That's right. I believe that by the time boys are seven or eight, they have begun to suspect that language is pretty much useless as a means of communicating. *Really* communicating, which is, *saying what you mean.* Boys are not stupid: all around them they see adults saying one thing and doing another.

But boys are not jaded and cynical either: they still *expect* people to talk truth, at least until enough adults in the family, the classroom, and the TV news have taught them otherwise. Hey, boys read the Founding Fathers' timeless phrases about liberty and justice for all, then learn those same dudes "owned" slaves. They watch as George Bush loudly insists his Supreme Court nominee is "the best qualified jurist in the nation," though the man has been a judge for a shorter time (sixteen months) than the average NFL placekicker holds a job. You think this gives boys confidence in speech? Oliver North gets up on TV and says, "Yes, I broke the law of the land and shredded the evidence, but *God bless America, land that I looooove* . . ." and he gets clean off! You telling me boys aren't able to conclude from this that lingo is bunco?

Boys also notice how infrequently adults listen to the words *boys* say, and how infrequently the orders that adults holler at them are really selected for personal, precise reasons. Boys see how much more eloquent an end-to-end rush on the soccer field is, in boy society, than a finely worded declaration of friendship. They cannot miss the ultimate point in all of this: words don't seem to amount to much.

So they carry on a kind of casual, careless test, a test that bobs along, nothing really serious: They curse each other, just throwing out a putdown here and an insult there, dropping in two-dollar words for emphasis. They trip along, evaluating the responses to their offhand negativity-that-is-not-really. And guess what? Nothing much happens. Saying "F— you, a—hole," to somebody instead of "Hey, Pete, what's up?" doesn't make much of a difference most of the time. Pete is as likely to say, "Oh, hey, Tony," as he is to say, "Kiss my b–tt, Dogbreath."

The allure of cussing and insulting wears off in a few years. Then the only boys who continue (especially into manhood) are the ones who actually *are* mean spirited and aggressive (yes, some of them are). Most other boys find other ways of using language for its minimally revealing purposes.

For example, they talk about sports all the time. Endless, intricate discussions of elaborate, subtle techniques and plays. A nonmale listening to them will conclude they are amazingly trivial and superficial, leading empty lives—but this is not so. They have learned language cannot reveal who they are by saying what they feel, so they are using a neutral topic—the designated-hitter rule, or the likelihood that America will ever be up to scratch in World Cup soccer—as a medium for intelligence and emotion. Believe me, we are listening to each other very carefully, and we are checking out each other's clearly perceivable evidence of style, memory, wit, smarts, temper, flexibility, loyalty, decisiveness, creativity, insight. The conclusions we draw from this evidence will lead to the evolution or curtailment of the relationship, whether it may be friendship, the purchase of a car, the decision to offer or accept a job, the decision about whether to welcome or resist a son-in-law . . .

BOOK: So, JL, I guess we've got it figured out pretty well here. Boys talk the way they do because they feel language is pretty useless and speech really means nothing. What do you think?

JL: Well, I don't know. I mean, maybe.

BOOK: Maybe? What is this "maybe" stuff, now? It's clear—language, speech, nothing! We've just been examining—

JL: Well, it depends, you know? On who is saying the nothing. And who is listening. Sometimes nothing says a lot. Sometimes, like—

BOOK: Never mind. Never mind, Dogbreath.

The Cap

First of all, it is not true that every boy wears a cap every minute he is awake. It sometimes looks that way, if you notice such things while looking out, say, over a sea of heads on an elementary school playground—but only because the eye tends to overlook the bare hairs in favor of those bobbing dots of the hot red and rich blue, the nasty-classy black, the rare and rather startling green (What is that guy, a Hartford Whalers fan or something? Green, possibly because it occurs so frequently in nature, is a terrible sports color. Check out the foul lanes at the Boston Garden sometime. Oogh.). There is plenty of hair, and no doubt most of it is very nice hair too, but it is extremely dull by comparison with caps.

The fact is, boys pretty much break down into those who would no more go outside without a cap than they would go outside without pants, and boys who cannot stand to have anything on their heads at all. This second group, as they mature, develop a kind of snotty attitude toward headgear, pretending to think boys who care about caps are vain and silly and worried about (ha!) catching cold or something. But this is not really how the anticaps feel, or at least this is not the reason they never developed a hat jones. The reason they never got into hats is that their mothers made them wear stupid ones. So they wouldn't catch cold.

There flat *are* some stupid hats manufactured for boys. Many of them—especially favored by mothers—feature pom-poms. (A pom-pom is one of those rare and wonderful items—some others are the Chihuahua, the flu, and the booger—that are fully as ridiculous and awful as their names imply.) What is it with pom-poms, anyway? What was the original purpose? I know why some shirts still have those little loops on the back—it's because people used to hang their shirts on hooks overnight, back in the sixteenth century when every male owned only two. But what was a pom-pom originally for, to give extremely maladroit people a woolly knob to grasp so they could pull their stocking hats off easily?

I'm certain that when a mother buys a stocking cap for her son, she doesn't even notice that it bears a pom-pom. She sees the hat and thinks, "That looks nice and warm! Johnny will never get a mean wicked ear infection if he wears that out to play every time he leaves the house between October and April!"

Never even sees the huge spongy ball bristling with gross cheap colors on the top, never even thinks of how it will bob in a little dipsy sort of motion with her kid's every step ("Hey guys, here comes cutie Flop-Top!"), never forms her lips and speaks the goofy word: *pom-pom*. To her, it's just part of the deal. But of course, when her son sees the hat all he notices is the you-know-what. So he sticks the hat in his book pack as soon as he turns the corner for school, or tosses it on the ground as an out-of-bounds marker for the playground football game, or does whatever he must to dissociate himself from it. And to him, alas, this is the agony of headgear.

The baseball cap is another story. It doesn't develop undignified countermotions on its own when you wear it—it perches where you put it, with a certain aloofness. You never feel you are *inside* such a cap, which somehow saves it from the uncomfortably snug intimacy of the stocking variety. The cap has a shape of its own, instead of merely highlighting the outline of your own head, which may be kind of bumpy and nothing you particularly want to show off. And although there are more and more caps with idiotic things occupying the space above the bill—I saw one the other day that said SCHUBERT; the only thing that would make this okay would be if the cap were orange, so you could look around in the morning and say, "Hey, has anybody seen my orange Schubert?"—for the most part these caps bear the names or logos of something associated with sports. These are, really, sports caps. And anything associated with sports is acceptable, even if it happens also to keep you from catching cold.

This is where we separate the men from the boys. Men seem to have forgotten the sports connection necessary to defend a piece of headwear. Men wear baseball caps that say any old thing (it was a man of about fifty who wore the Schubert cap, which was, by the way, yellow. Yellow!). Pick out thirty men wearing caps, and aside from three or four sports caps you'll get:

- Five or six with logos associated with fishing (fishing is not a sport; fishing is just fishing);
- Five or six with logos associated with trucking (boys have not yet been warped by office jobs into considering truck drivers the ultimate romantic real men of our culture; mostly they imagine that the people who drive huge trucks around the clock on endless trips must be bored and tired);
- Seven or eight with the logos of resorts (OLÉ CANCUN! Caps bearing the names of golf courses, or anything else associated with golf, must be classified as resort caps);
- Two or three with purely personal messages (MCGINTY FAMILY REUNION 1984 or I ♡ JESUS);
- Eight or nine—the largest group—with logos advertising some company or product (DIET COKE, JUST FOR THE TASTE OF IT! or everybody's favorite, NIKE, with the little swoopy line).

Boys would never choose to wear any of these caps. Why would you let a sneaker company advertise itself on your head when you could have CAROLINA or RAIDERS there instead? And although I myself would find a cap with the word ZEBCO on it kind of appealing in and of itself, as an item adorned by a very fine-sounding word that only incidentally happens to be the name of a fishing-reel manufacturer, I know most boys would put it on their heads only if it said ZEBCO HOCKEY or something like that. And I don't blame them.

I should add that boys do not wear caps touting their favorite sports teams because they fantasize about belonging to that team. Caps are not costume gear for Walter Mitty dreams ("Hey, I'm Cal Ripken, and here's the pitch . . ."). Boys do fantasize like this sometimes, but the cap has nothing to do with it. Instead, it's a matter of simply demonstrating an affiliation based on loyalty, to the game in question as well as to the team. My son has five Orioles caps—differently designed—that demonstrate his loyalty to baseball in general and to the Baltimore club in particular. What makes him pick one over the other on this day or that is less important than the fact that there is continuity. He also has a Mariners cap (gift from a friend in Seattle) and an Astros hat (friend in Houston) and a Yankees cap (fool of a friend in New York), and although he never wears any of these, he insists on keeping them every time his mother tries to clean off the cap shelf. They affirm the baseball feeling, and make his choice of the O's all the more overt. Alex also has three Washington Capitals caps, against only a single rather perfunctory Redskins cap that is almost never worn, reflecting his conviction (and mine, too—see it spelled out on page 76) that our city is too football crazy at the expense of its hockey yeomen. And when I come home from a trip with a souvenir weird small-franchise cap for him—from Colorado College hockey, for example, or Rochester Red Wings minor-league baseball—he wears it intensively for a few weeks, savoring its curiosity value. But for all of its strangeness, it is still just a sports cap.

Unlike Jim Courier's cap. Perhaps the most startlingly noticeable athletic cap in the world, but it is not a true sports cap! This gets pretty technical, so follow closely. Tennis is definitely a sport; Jim Courier, a major stud tennis player, is definitely a sportsman. He wears a cap when he plays tennis. Therefore, it must be a sports cap, right?

Wrong, for several reasons. Because tennis is a sport without a cap tradition—unlike baseball—a cap's use must be studied. Courier's does not pass. First, it is a plain white cap. White! No logo, no word, nothing. Where did he even *find* it? Looks like something a dentist would wear to keep the sun out of his eyes while he performed oral surgery outdoors. Which is pretty much why Courier wears it, actually—bringing us to the second reason it's not a sports cap: It serves a purpose. Your true sports cap is worn by boys for nothing that could be called a purpose—a cap cannot be justified by simple, practical reasons. Yes, there is a hint of wanting to look good, and a hint, maybe, of wanting to cover the head if, say, it's sleeting outside (though many a boy won't wear a good cap under such conditions; don't want to mess up a good cap with sleet). But a nice appearance or a dry, cool scalp really doesn't come close to the vague complex of reasons a boy reaches for a cap. So Courier, who won the 1993 Australian Open on a court where the nearly tropical sun raised the temperature to 153 degrees, against a capless Stefan Edberg, is no boy's cap idol. He has every good reason in the world to wear his cap. Therefore, he is a duck, and no respectable boy in America is going to start wearing a dentist cap any more than he would wear a pom-pom ski cap in February.*

On a recent late spring morning, Alex and I stood for some moments in front of the cap shelf before walking over to the school bus stop, seriously studying the options, whizzing through the factors determining choice in our heads on the same non-

---

*NEWS FLASH: By the time Wimbledon 1993 rolled around, Courier had traded in his dentist cap for a sneaker-logo squiggle. It is *still* not a sports cap, and it's still ugly.

verbal level that provides feelings about a song on the radio or a condiment on a sandwich. Suddenly his mother came downstairs and saw us and said, "Oh, it's warm enough today that you don't need to wear a hat, Alex!"

She was beaming—she felt good about this offer, freeing him from her usual fussiness about head coverings, giving him a gift, really, a liberation. The gaiety in her voice was touching. Alex looked up, forced a wan smile at her, and flicked a panicky glance at me. It was a tense moment. Should he swallow hard and take her up on it, just so that she could enjoy what she imagined was a benevolent gesture? Would repelling her offer—by wearing a cap anyway—spoil her cap-kindness for the future, when he might really be grateful for it—on a warmish winter day, for example, when she might let him downgrade from wool hat to cap without a struggle?

Or, on the other hand, was appearing in school without a cap just too terrible a prospect?

I could see how torn he was. His eyes pleaded with me: Think of something! It was plainly one of those moments when a man has to step forward and be a father. I grabbed an O's cap—the black one with the ornithologically correct bird that we got on Cap Day, 1989—as if it were for myself and said, "Okay, we'd better go."

Alex breathed easily despite being bareheaded, thanked his mom with a cheery smile, and we left.

As soon as we got around the corner he grabbed the cap from me and put it on. Immediately he seemed a little ashamed of what might be construed as vanity, even though I am a cap wearer too. He squinted into the air around him as if sensing its subtlest portents. He said, "Frankly, it's not all *that* warm."

Risky Pals

There's a kid in your school whom you have heard of and noticed, a kid who maybe once pulled some stunt that was bad but kind of cool (and therefore much discussed), a kid who is known for getting into more than a few scraps, a kid who some lesser guys adore in a goony way, who some prissy guys hate, who some tough guys are a little scared of, but who seems mostly to hang by himself. Probably he is good at sports in a ferocious sort of way, tearing into the game but holding himself aloof from yippee-yippee celebrations on the field. Teachers do not like this guy. He doesn't much like them, either. He gets into little bits of trouble— nothing major, but a constant series of wearying small hassles. This stuff makes you uneasy, but watching him now and then, you sense something more interesting than simple badness. Some flickers of seriousness, and some moments when he lets himself get humorous in a way that doesn't cut anybody. You are not ready to approve or disapprove, but you definitely find him intriguing. Then one day he comes up to you to talk or do something routine, and you go along, a little flattered, very curious, and much less apprehensive than you would have thought; then it happens more and more; then one day you notice you are with him more than anybody else is. Then, finally, you realize you are pretty much his only friend.

If you are a Good Kid, the teachers may look on your new bond with a little concern. So may your parents. If they know the boy's reputation, or if they sense his troublesome nature when they meet him, they may even ask you close questions about the time you spend with him. Your pal—let's call him Eric— seems at first to be tamer than usual when he is in your company, and you tell your parents this. They consider the information, and, because you don't seem to be unwilling to acknowledge the faults in Eric's usual behavior, they trust your insight. You really like Eric by now, and they can tell.

Secretly, you think that maybe you are even kind of a help to him—maybe your safer, more orderly ways will teach him better methods of dealing with the deeper trouble that you see more than ever in him. You hate to be grandiose about yourself, but you do think that you are possibly a Good Example for Eric. Maybe this is why he was drawn to you— this, and the fact that you have never been judgmental. Almost everyone disapproved of Eric; you didn't, and he figured it out. You are pleased.

However, as the two of you spend more time together, things begin to change a little. Eric starts to loosen up. He says and does things that creep toward being troublesome. You force yourself not to pull back; you stick with him, slightly increasing the goodness you beam at him to draw him away from bad inclinations. But it doesn't work. He gets less inhibited. Your parents ask you routinely about how he is doing, and you continue to assure them everything is great. But everything is not great; you are increasingly uncomfortable in Eric's company.

Eric, however, is increasingly comfortable in yours. He lets himself go more often, and obviously presumes you are with him in his actions. Once, when he is doing something kind of carelessly destructive—breaking some bottles you found, by throwing them against a building, say, or teasing a dog inside a fence by twitching at it with a stick—you say something to indicate your disapproval. He looks at you with a flash of disappointment, perhaps even contempt. He seems, for just a flash, very alone again. You hastily cover up your concern. The troublesome actions resume, and go on, and get worse.

You want to talk to your parents, but you feel uneasy doing so. First, you would have to admit to them that you misjudged Eric: He was not as easily converted to Good Boyness as you thought. This would hurt, because you are proud that your parents tend to trust your judgment. (You also would have to admit to yourself that perhaps you are not as powerful in your positivity as you thought. This, too, hurts.)

Second, you are certain your parents wouldn't understand the complexity of the situation, the nearness of Eric to being okay, the fact that he can still be pulled away from serious trouble; you know your parents would simply insist that you remove yourself from the potential problems. They would be shocked by the surface badness of what Eric does. They wouldn't see through it. You would have to drop Eric, and then what would he do?

Third, they might even feel the need to report Eric's actions to his parents, or an authority at school, or the police. This would be a disaster.

But the more you think about it—and the worse Eric's behavior gets—the more you find yourself wondering if it might not be a good thing if someone caught Eric at one of his tricks. Not your parents, and not anyone to whom you "tattled," for you would never tattle; but someone else, who doesn't know the subtleties, but who simply makes Eric face what he is doing. You feel horribly disloyal for such thoughts, especially because Eric's acts are getting more serious, justifying more serious punishment if he were ever caught.

One day, Eric throws a rock at a school bus driving by and hits it. The two of you run; you are *pretty* sure the bus driver did not see you. A couple of days later, in his neighborhood, Eric purposefully breaks a wine bottle he has found and places large pieces of glass beneath the tires of a parked car belonging to a person he says he needs to get back at for yelling at him a couple of weeks ago. Later, after you have both gone home for the night, you sneak back and remove the glass. As you are walking home in the dark, your relief suddenly turns cold as you realize: What would have happened if the car's owner had come out and found . . . you? What if it is you—and not Eric—who gets caught? You who has to face the consequences of what Eric is doing?

Well, this is a sticky business for you and your parents, too. There are lots of Good Boys out there and lots of Not-Quite-Bad Boys, and they tend to find each other and hold on. Every GB has within him a sense of fascinated compassion for the mysterious problems and hidden strengths of the NQBB; every NQBB recognizes true goodness when he sees it in respectable form—in another boy, that is, not in an assistant principal's lecture—and secretly wants some of it to rub off. Good Boys are not above craving a few moments in the wicked darkness they know is not really their place. Not Quite Bads are not below craving some sincere approval from teachers and the like.

So the Good Boy picks up a few chills and thrills, a touch of worldliness, and a toughish self-reliance, while the Not-Quite-Bad Boy learns to hear the voice inside that says "Don't do it!" and relax with the ensuing restraint, without fear of being a wimp. Both gain, both remain themselves. It's a perfect match, almost an inevitable one.

Ideally, that is. If the goodness rubs off on the tough guy early enough, it can forestall the increasingly bad acts in the later stages. Or, if the self-reliance rubs off early enough on the good guy, it can fortify him to stand firm against some proposed malfeasance. In such cases, the friendship can turn into the best either boy could have, and it can grow and last forever.

Sure, it *can*. It *might*. If everything goes just right, if the aspects that are different make each kid come closer to his pal, make him want to tell the world "He's not what you all think."

But more often the things that are different make the boys pull away from each other. This, after all, is a natural way we deal with differences. And then, each kid begins to seem awful, and it becomes easy for the goodie to say, "He's just a dangerous jerk," and for the baddie to say, "He's just a wuss." This is the most common defense in the world: I'm okay, he's not. I'm bigger because he's smaller. I'm right because he's wrong.

As always, this defense stinks. All it really does is point out that the person using it does not believe in himself—and in fact may believe exactly what the other person is saying. The Good Boy *does* fear he's a wimp. The Not-Quite-Bad Boy *does* worry that he'll end up doing something horrible that will land him in jail. So for the record, let's get a few things straight.

It's okay to be a Good Boy. A kid who has excellent sense and virtuous values; who likes the kind of orderliness that depends on authority; who is uncomfortable hurting the feelings of other people, even the dopes and nerds in his class; who squirms when rules are aggressively broken; this kind of boy is *not* automatically a wussy, wimpy, no-balls weakling. All such Good Boys—even the ones with immense self-confidence and Quiet Strength—are always wondering if maybe they are hopeless prigs. (No! You are *not!*)

A Good Boy is still just a boy. Parents and teachers rightfully appreciate guys with integrity and discernment, and they want such kids to enjoy this appreciation—through reinforcement, rewards, and increased trust and responsibility. This is all great, unless the Good Boy begins to feel two things: first, that he has too much to live up to, which makes him try harder, and second, that he appeals too much to adults and not enough to other kids.

A Not-Quite-Bad Boy is still just a boy, too. Teachers and parents should be able to keep this in mind. They can recognize the difference between a warped kid who is nothing but trouble—a Really-Bad Boy— and a fairly well-balanced kid who is driven by some interior fizz to nibble and pick away at rules, feelings, and order in general. The problem is, the Not-Quite-Bad Boy can quickly become much more of a pain in the pants than the truly Bad Boy. The Bad Boy generally does something manifestly awful, often huge; the reprisal from authority is equally potent and absolute: The Bad Boy is shut down. The Not Quite never quite provokes such a satisfying body slam of negation, so the exasperation builds up. Pretty soon the kid is picking away, and the adults are picking away back. As the picks get more frequent they grow to seem continuous. Habit sets in; the hard work of stepping back and treating the boy gently on those occasions when he merits it becomes more and more difficult. (Just so, for the boy, does the hard work of stepping back and admitting the teacher or parent has a good point once in while.)

Adults tend to count on boys having a clear trouble alarm, that little bell that goes off in the head when you creep up on doing something that is going to get you into trouble. It is true that most boys do hear the bell, and most then look for a way out, because they don't *want* trouble. GBs tend to be more highly alert in this way, and NQBBs usually know when something's wrong too, though they may be more careless. However, hearing the bell doesn't mean you're going to heed the warning. Tempting trouble is one way of dancing on the edge of the dark, and this gives the NQBB a little jolt of life, especially as more and more adults act sterner and sterner toward him. His alarm bell gets so it rings pretty much all the time; naturally he stops really hearing it.

Soon, because of habit, carelessness, and curiosity, his sense of the edge is lost. He's in the dark.

One way out is to talk to somebody. Almost any adult would say, "Hey, he can talk to me! I'm here for him!" but adults really forget how difficult it is for boys to trust them. Especially the NQBB, who will be essentially confessing some bad stuff that most adults will feel compelled to punish. It is probably true that most NQBBs got into their rather twisty condition in the first place because they lacked people they trusted.

It would seem to be a lot easier for the Good Boy to trust adults, but it's not. Adults all consider themselves Good Grownups, especially as compared to boys, but boys don't buy it. The qualities of Goodness do not accrue automatically with age. Even if they did, even if all adults were wonderful human beings, there is no guarantee they can be trusted as listeners. Listening to a boy requires all kinds of discernment and restraint, in addition to the more obvious tools of precise inquiry and empathy. GBs are as careful as anyone about assessing these in advance. The GB almost always *wants* to discuss the problem of a risky friendship, but he knows it is perilously easy for a parent to hear the first few danger signals and react with all the subtlety of an ambulance.

If a kid wants to discuss a troubled friend with one of his parents, it is because he wants to understand something, not because he wants to blow the whistle. But even though he is looking to the parent ultimately for some kind of insight, he is also aware that *he* knows his Not-Quite-Bad friend much better than the parent does, even though the parent may have been overtly watching and analyzing for months. Parents tend to try to take over the friend—that is, to turn a complex, intimately known kid into some Type We Know All About and Must Now Handle. This kind of imperialism wrecks everything.

By far the harder task for a parent is proving he or she can keep a secret. This is the nitty-gritty of trustworthiness; this is what even the Best Boys are skittish about. Parents are not good at sitting on shocking revelations, especially when it seems sharing the news would bring help for the troubled kid.

My son Alex has a Not-Quite-Bad pal who used to be just kind of a smartass but snapped into a sharp turn toward trouble last year after his parents' divorce. I like this kid. He is smart, quick, funny, and athletic. But it is clear he can turn all of his smarts into shrewd mischief, his quickness into recklessness, and his humor into nasty mockery in a flash. I've kept my eye on the friendship. My wife took one look at the kid and wanted simply to forbid Alex to play with him. This shows the good sense that is typical of my wife, and the tendency to amputate that is often typical of her gender. Moms say, "Why bother? Nip it off now." I kept making excuses to my wife for leaving the friendship to ripen a bit, promising that Alex would let me know if anything bad was coming.

Fortunately, Alex did so. He led up to the revelations gradually, starting with petty stuff. One day he would casually mention a new phrase of cursing his pal was trying out these days and watch to see if I reacted with sternness or fear of infection; another time he'd say, "Bruce, did you ever like to ring people's doorbells and run away when you were my age?" or "What do you think of someone who hides in the bushes and says 'F— you, you f—ing jerk!' when an adult walks by, and then runs?"

What indeed? Well, I kept my nervousness to myself. The talks began to broaden in scope. Alex wanted to know if the kid's behavior, which now included a fascination with fighting, revealed that the kid was basically unhappy. I said I supposed it did. Was it all from the divorce? No, but the divorce probably heated things up. Alex wanted to know about what happens to kids' feelings when their parents divorce. We discussed it (my parents were divorced when I was six; Alex had read a story I wrote about it). He began to bring more and more of his friend's behavior into the talk, providing pieces of the whole that was taking shape for him. By now there was no more pretense of impersonal action ("What if a kid . . ."); the smashings and deceptions were attributed openly to his friend. And some of them were pretty serious, acts that would get the kid—and Alex along with him—into trouble with the law. A line had been crossed in the past few weeks, out of "boy stuff" into the lower levels of the world men were supposed to be responsible for.

Now I had a problem. Alex had revealed the commission of actual petty crimes to me. My stuffy sense of the Good Grownup's social responsibility demanded to know: Wasn't I obligated to report them? Well, I didn't think so; I mean, up to a point I think society is capable of protecting itself from eleven-year-old malefactors. Okay, then, simply as a fellow father, shouldn't I let the kid's dad know what was going on? This sense of obligation was not so easily put down. I knew the dad, and he was a responsible, supportive father. But I had the feeling he didn't have any idea of what his son was really doing. Obviously, I should fill him in.

I told Alex what I was thinking—that the things he was describing took him and his friend outside the equivocal area of parental discipline into the rigid realm of (gulp) police justice, where dads were powerless to bestow leniency; that the inner trouble such acts revealed probably required some kind of (gulp) treatment. It was time, wasn't it, to break the news?

Alex's reaction was immediate, simple, and clear: "No way!" He had told me in confidence; how could I consider breaking that? He had me there; how, indeed, could I think of it? All I could muster from my fading sense of adult responsibility was a false-sounding, formal request that he release me from the secrecy "for the sake of" his friend. He thought for a minute. He said, "No."

Whoa! Alex was willing to nix the possibility that his friend could be helped; to preserve his own integrity, to keep on feeling he was the kind of kid who could keep a secret, Alex would draw the line and say, "Now it's *his* problem." It took a minute for me to understand this, but I got it. You have to get what's good for *you* out of a friendship, even out of its problems. There is nothing especially exploitative in this; it's just the way giving and taking work. If you are a bighearted, generous person, you will be a patient friend, taking the long view of another kid, working things out along the way to the rewarding amity you anticipate. If you are a gimme-it-now person, you will pick up and drop friends more quickly, calibrating your efforts to match the immediate payoffs. In both cases, you are guided by an essential selfishness that is, well, natural. It is also kind of a secret we keep to ourselves.

So I told Alex he was right—I would keep my mouth shut. All the secrets would be safe. No new provisions would be made, no punitive or cautious limitations placed on the friendship. We would not bring the secrets to the surface by turning them into acts.

But once the truth has been acknowledged, even privately, it has a way of finding its way into action. I don't know what small things began to happen between Alex and his friend, but I suspect the boy began to sniff out Alex's growing resolution. This would lead, of course, to resentment, sarcasm, lonesomeness—a whole sequence of strains pulling in opposite directions. I don't know the details, but I'm sure a lot was going on, because the other day, the kid picked a fight with Alex during a football game, and persisted in trying to pound Alex time and time again after the fight had been broken up several times. Other kids in the neighborhood came to tell me about it; when Alex himself came home he said only, "There was a fight." He wasn't hurt, but he was subdued.

Later that night he announced to me that he was going to stop seeing the boy for a while. "I've got to protect myself," he said morosely, sitting on his bed. I should have felt like celebrating: Teaching your son that he's got to protect himself is one of the most fundamental and difficult duties a dad faces, and here I was seeing my kid teach it to himself. But I can tell you: When they teach themselves, boys learn the hard way. The pain and grim dignity are awesome. And compared to what his son is learning, it ought to be pretty easy for a father to learn to keep his mouth shut when it counts.

Bullies

Author's Personal Disclaimer

L et me begin by saying that bullies are scum and it is okay to hate them. A big kid picking on a small kid forfeits all claim to any sort of redeeming quality. I know some boys who are nice guys when they are not engaged in acts of bullying, and I can admit that during those times they are okay and I would probably *not* send them straight to the bottom of the sea in a trash bag full of sand. At such times I can even hope they may be cured of bullying and grow up to be good citizens. But when they are engaged in acts of bullying, forget it: I don't *want* them to grow up; I want them to disappear. If I had a Mega-Martian Molecular-Destructo Vaporizer Ray Gun, I would use it again and again, grimly but happily, to turn them all into smoke.

I know, I know—these are shockingly harsh words,

especially for someone who considers himself a bighearted, socially compassionate, ingeniously understanding, nonjudgmental sort of fellow, and an adult to boot, who is ready to forgive those who trespass against me and my family, especially when the trespasser is a child. But there is something about a bully that negates my spirit of even basic human generosity. Bullies have caused me, and now my son, enough undeserved pain that I am willing to judge them all right now: They suck.

I guess I am about to write about bullies so that all of us might understand them better. But I do so with a pretty cold heart. Maybe in a few pages we will all feel more forgiving, and I suppose that would be grand. But right now I protest in advance: An understanding of bullies should never be used to take even the tiniest step toward a justification of bullies. The only reason I want anyone to understand bullies is so they can *defeat* bullies. Defeat them well.

History and Background

It seems there have always been bullies. Certainly you can find them in old texts and legends—Greek tales, African myths, the Upanishads, Charles Dickens novels. Several of the Roman gods were not above pushing relatively powerless humans around to amuse themselves. Samson was probably a bully as a kid, and Goliath too, though by the time we get to stories about them in the Bible their roughness was sanctioned: They were warriors, they were supposed to fight, even when their opponents were smaller. Goliath, of course, got what we want all bullies to get in an unfair fight ("Surprise, big fella!"), whereas Samson took on a thousand soldiers and killed them all with the jawbone of a donkey. A guy who jumps into a thousand-against-one battle cannot really be called a bully, though he probably has a certain problem with arrogance. A bully would never take on a fight at such odds, even if he swung a mean bone.

The defining fact about a bully is that he selects a weaker person to pick on. This, of course, is a weak act, which really means the bully is himself a weakling. Some clever social-work theorist could now point out that the physical weakness of the victim is matched by the moral weakness of the bully—which makes the fight fair after all, weakling against weakling. (Some clever social-work theorists also say the only problem with drugs is that they are illegal. Next question.)

And anyway, the fight is only fair if there *is* a fight. There usually isn't, because that's another thing about bullies: They don't want to fight. They want only to intimidate. Now, normal people can't understand what the thrill is in intimidation—although we'll give it a try here in a few minutes—but a social worker, or better yet a lawyer, could point out that at least intimidation is technically nonviolent. A fifth grader who lightly bumps a third grader into a locker and jeers at him and shakes his fist in his small face is not actually breaking bones or drawing blood. No harm, no foul, right? So intimidation must be preferable to actual fisticuffs; bullies are better than brawlers, yes?

No. Brawlers are dangerous jerks in their own way, but at least they put their badness on the line. They risk losing, and often they do, usually to another brawler. There's a certain self-respect in a kid who likes to fight; he will choose an antagonist who looks like an equal. He'll skip over all the little guys and bespectacled math geniuses and no-clue wussies in the school and go after another tough guy. Whereas the bully will hide from the tough ones, and prey only on the smaller and younger. The bully hopes desperately he will *never* get in a fight, so he daunts only people who are not likely to give him one. The great secret about the bully is that he stinks as a fighter. He can be had. That is probably one reason he became a bully in the first place.

Modern Origins

I am certain a lot of bullies are bullied in their homes. Their fathers or stepfathers yell at them and push them around, or their brothers do, or their mom's boyfriends do. (I don't really think a rough mom will turn a boy into a bully—I think it's a guy deal. I do think having a mom who is pushed around by a guy contributes, though.) The neighborhood bully who has tormented my son Alex since they were eight and six, respectively, gets yelled at a lot by a huge, ill-tempered, profane dad. Often, the curses this kid uses with Alex are obviously borrowed directly from his father; once, for example, he kept telling Alex, "F— you and your whole f—ing generation!" If it weren't so sad, it would be funny: an eight-year-old cursing the generation of a six-year-old. Another favorite curse—for a long time—has been equally revealing: this kid calls Alex "You f—ing bitch!" No boy calls another boy that. But if he hears his father screaming that all the time at his mother . . .

This father—let's call him Mervin—is an unusually corrupt case, in that he proclaims outright, even rather proudly, that he sees nothing wrong with an older, bigger kid shoving a younger, smaller kid around ("If your little wimp is younger than my son, that's his problem," says Mervin). But the fact is, most fathers do teach their sons that picking on younger or even smaller boys is taboo. It's a basic rule of manhood: Don't mess with someone weaker than you. That's for cowards.

However, the next time such a good-preaching dad loses his temper, he very well may proceed to screw up the lesson completely—by using his full advantage of strength, authority, and language to daunt a younger, smaller, weaker male who happens to be his son. The son is then faced with a choice: He can consider his father a coward and a hypocrite, or he can consider the rule to be flexible, if not false.

This is a no-brainer for the boy. None of us wants to think of our dad as a coward and hypocrite, even if our dad has just screamed at us or knocked us down. We would prefer to take the option that allows us to preserve some respect for our dad, so we choose to believe the don't-mess-with-littler-guys rule is kind of bogus. This works, doesn't it? An eight-year-old who has just been picked on by a thirty-two-year-old will certainly see nothing particularly awful in picking on another kid only a couple of years younger than himself. The unfairness ratio of 8 to 6 is nothing compared to that of 32 to 8. So why bother restraining the urge to terrorize an only-slightly-weaker guy?

I said in the first paragraph of this chapter that I wouldn't care if all bullies were vaporized. Perhaps I should give them the following chance: Let their bully fathers be vaporized first, and then see if the kids get better. (You can start with Mervin.)

Where You Find Bullies

Everywhere, it seems. If there are twenty groups of boys, in nineteen of them at least one of the bigger kids will want to act like a tough guy to one of the littler ones.

But let's be very clear about one thing: Bullies do *not* automatically arise in every group as a natural function of male society. People expound theories claiming this, but the theories are sloppy and wrong. Bullies are boys with particular character traits, and if your soccer team or Sunday school class doesn't happen to contain a guy with those traits, you're in the clear: another kid who lacks them will *not* suddenly become a bully to fill the void. Because bullies are so plentiful, acting up all over the place, we can mistake frequency for universality.

It is true that in every group of boys—and I do mean every one—there will be some competing, some challenging, some testing of strength or resolve. But this kind of contention, even if it gets a bit rough, is different from bullying. Sometimes this sort of testing even suppresses bullying. Bullies check out their environments very carefully, and if a bully sees that all the guys around him can take care of themselves and won't stand for any mess, he will lie dormant. But when a smaller or younger or weaker kid joins the group—a new kid in school, for example—the bully will go to work on him.

Two things are necessary for a bully to show up in a group of boys: first, the bully himself—a kid who wants to intimidate a pushover victim—and second, a pushover victim. If a group is missing either of these, the group will be free from bullying.

What's In It for the Bully?
Beats me. The life of a bully seems like an awful lot of trouble. You have to be extremely cautious and sneaky, first in picking out a victim who you feel sure won't stand up to you, and second in practicing your tough-guy stuff on him without arousing any

defense—from him, from the adults who hover around, or, most important, from the normal boys among whom you and your victim conduct your lives.

Normal boys are disgusted by bullying, but they will usually allow a certain low level of it to go on in front of them. Their tolerance is not really dishonorable; boys just naturally give other boys some slack to work out their own problems without too much interference. But if a bully pushes too hard— gets too nasty to his victim or acts too triumphant in the group at large, as if tormenting a weak kid really proved anything—the latent honor of the normal boys will be called upon, and they will drop the bully into his place for the moment. Almost always, this is done perfunctorily, with distaste rather than personal anger or passion—a weary "Leave the kid alone, asshole," or "Hey, there are some of us here your own size you could pick on, you know"—and the terms of the protest are clearly implied to be limited. The bully knows that if he retreats for a short time, and then enacts his torment a little more discreetly, he will be allowed to resume and continue until once again his obnoxiousness gets too obvious to ignore.

One reason normal guys don't act with greater firmness is their perplexity. They simply don't understand what the thrill might be that a bully supposedly gets out of his perversion. The behavior is so weird, and so disgraceful, that they don't want to come too close. Frankly, I cannot understand the thrill either. I guess it's two things at once: the thrill of using power, and the wicked liberty of discarding the scolding, internal restrictions of conscience and honor. Power is something boys almost never get to exercise; conscience is something they are forced to exercise all too often.

Which brings us to the worst part of what I imagine the life of the bully to be, far more agonizing than the sneaking and risking: A bully has to do something he knows is wrong. Yes, he does *too* know. I don't care how rough his home life is, how feckless his guardians are in passing on the code of manhood, how stupid he himself may be—he *knows* it is wrong to bust the chops of a little kid. He *knows* it is weak. He *knows* he is a wuss, even if he has a fool of a dad like Mervin telling him it's okay, go ahead, no problem, be a tough guy in a tough world, kick the ass of anyone you can. This knowledge must be a terrible thing to live with. Somehow, I can imagine that by doing it more—bullying more and more kids—you can pretend it's less intense a disgrace, it's just a habit, it's no big deal, it's just the way you are. But I don't believe bullies really fool themselves. They are miserable.

And once I have felt sufficiently sorry for all the kids they torment, once I have seen all those kids throw off the effects of being intimidated and hurt all the time, once I have seen the victims' misery brought to a complete end without any consequences—well, then, perhaps I will have a smidgen of sympathy left over for the bullies. In the meantime, I'd rather encourage them to change in the only way they readily understand.

What to Do About Bullies

How about punching them in the nose?

I hate to say it, but making bullies look bad in books and movies does not seem to be an effective deterrent, though it gives us peace-loving adult guys a nice tingle of revenge for the agonies we suffered as kids and later as fathers. I daresay every bully who has appeared in print or on the screen, in every book or movie from the Bible to *Tom Sawyer,* from *Way Down East* to *Stand by Me,* shows himself to be a totally repulsive, ugly-hearted, morally indecent, stupid fiend. The writers and film directors of the world have never gotten confused about this one. But who have we convinced? When we kill off a nasty bully in the last chapter and imagine that we are teaching the children of the world something ("Take that!"), we are obviously wrong. Either the children we should be reaching are not paying attention, or—most likely—they are laughing raucously (as they steal candy from the wee Nice Child sitting to their left).

Telling on a bully just after he has struck is usually a waste of breath. A teacher cannot police a bully all the time; the bully will just pick his spots more carefully. Also, most teachers don't really understand the subtlety and relentlessness of a bully's nibbling. They will react if the bully overtly punches his prey, and they will take this big manifestation of violence as the ultimate problem. Well, first of all, most bullies aren't foolish enough to bop a little kid in front of a teacher, and second, even if they do, this is not the final move in their endgame—it is just another gambit in an endless series of moves.

Going a level higher and talking, say, to the school principal about the long-term problem can be effective sometimes. You have to be coherent and prepared to present the bully's action as a determined series of small attacks. Keep in mind that each isolated bump or shove doesn't sound so bad; it is only when they are seen as parts of a long, relentless torment that they look serious. The school probably has some kind of policy for dealing with bullies (remember, bullies are nothing new). Whether it works or not depends on a lot of variables: how smart the policy is, how good the principal is, how much or how little the bully is inclined to listen to adults, even when they threaten him, and so on.

You should also try talking to your father (or big brother). Perhaps you hesitate because he is a macho sort of guy and you are ashamed to tell him that you have been letting another boy push you around. Don't be; even if your father acts disappointed and angry that you haven't been macho yourself, keep in mind that *he* ain't the one getting poked and punched by a big kid; the bully doesn't look so big to *him*, but you know better. Try to get your father to help you figure out if there is any peaceful way to get the bully to lay off. He may have some ideas.

But don't get your hopes up. Talking to bullies rarely makes them do anything but scoff. They believe only in power. The only way to get through to them may be to show them a little power of your own. You might just have to punch your bully in the nose.*

Whew. I hate saying this, because it amounts to proposing violence, and I feel guilty proposing violence. I would far rather offer some peaceful deal you could entreat a bully to accept. But peaceful deals with bullies only stay peaceful on one side. Bullies *love* peaceful deals—they love to have their victims promise not to do anything physical. So, I'm afraid that sometimes your only choice is to hit the sucker. But don't worry—once will probably be enough, and it's almost certain he will not hit back. If he does, he's an oddball. I hope it doesn't hurt too much. But even if it does, you can be comfortable with the knowledge that he will probably leave you alone from now on.

There are some preliminary steps to take before you decide to strike. These won't do much, but they will at least convince you (and your teachers and

---

*If weapons are involved—if the bully has a knife or a gun—he is no longer just a bully. He is a potential killer. Report him, immediately, and *STAY AWAY*.

your parents) that you have made a sincere effort to stop the bullying through reasonable, peaceful means.

The first step is to hold several truths in your mind. They might make you a little more comfortable with the prospect of striking back at the big guy who is ruining your life.

1. Bullies are cowards. They are weak, weak, weak.
2. Bullies do not want to fight you. They just want to make you *think* they will gladly fight you.
3. Bullies carefully select victims they are sure won't fight back. They want to mess only with pushovers. If you show that you are not such a pushover, the bully will prefer to move on to another victim who is.
4. Bullies are generally very cagey about selecting people to pick on, and they pay attention to their surroundings. If you stand up to one bully in your school, for example, the other bullies will know about it and they will leave you alone in the future.
5. Bullies are not skilled fighters. They are only skilled at making threats to fight.

Now are we feeling much better? Well, probably not; this is a grim, scary business, and all the rah-rah mental preparation in the world cannot slow your pounding heart when you stand there and decide to ball your fist and clonk the villain. What *will* make you feel a little better is some technique and some practice. Your father or brother can show you how to throw a quick jab from a good defensive stance. You can master the punch on your own, so that when the time comes, you can be decisive, swift, and courageous.

But still—it's pretty awful. Why do we have to go through this? No one can say what it is about males that brings every boy to this brink sometime in his childhood, but we all stand up and step across at some point. We can only hope once is enough. Alas, bullies are not likely to disappear as a subspecies; like mosquitoes, they keep showing up and buzzing around the edges of life, without giving a clue as to why Nature made them and put them in our path. Perhaps they serve the oblique purpose of teaching us we can face something we fear, and stand up to it, and, if absolutely necessary, fight back. It's a good lesson to learn, certainly. Maybe we ought to be grateful for the rather perverse opportunity. Maybe when the bully is lying on the ground looking up at us with utter shock in his eyes, holding a hand to his bleeding nose, starting to cry, we ought to smile down at him, raise a friendly hand, and say "Thanks, chump."

Questions
for the Gunners

1. Do you need a gun to frighten people, or do you need it to shoot people?
2. If you didn't have a gun, would the other people who have guns notice you? Is being noticed safer, or more dangerous?
3. Is the gun itself, silent and at peace, beautiful?
4. If so, is it still beautiful when it shoots?
5. If not, what happens? Do you wonder at the loss?
6. Do you always want a new gun?
7. The power you get from having a gun—do you feel it even when the gun is not in use? When the gun is not with you?
8. Do others sense the power you get from the gun when you don't have it?
9. Do you feel less and less that this power stays with you when you are not holding the gun?
10. If so, do you feel more and more that the power

really isn't in you at all, but is entirely in the gun?

11. If so, do you find you want to use it more?
12. Do you shoot people when you are angry?
13. If so, does the anger go away?
14. Do you shoot people when you are cold?
15. If so, do you stay cold?
16. Do you feel like laughing at the person you shoot?
17. If the person you shoot dies, do you feel friendly toward him now?
18. Do you resent him?
19. Are you sometimes afraid of the gun?
20. Are you sometimes afraid of yourself?
21. Would you like it better if no one but you had a gun?
22. Would you prefer that everyone had a gun?
23. Would you prefer that no one had a gun?
24. Do you ever think about shooting yourself?
25. Does anyone deserve to be shot?
26. Does everyone deserve to be shot?
27. Does it matter, deserving to be shot?
28. One day, when you look at the gun, does it look like a stranger?
29. One day, when you pick up the gun, does it weigh too little?
30. One day, does it weigh too much?
31. Now that you have a gun, will there ever be a time when you will choose not to have a gun?

Stink

The other day I was walking around the house with my one-month-old son Spencer, inhaling the fine little aroma that rose off his warm scalp. It was not, of course, the odious candy-coo scent that chemical companies have decided is The Baby Smell, the one they put into every product you will ever bring near a baby: towelettes, diapers, lotions, shampoos, powders, cotton swabs, teething toys, even some baby books. Heck, even some *parent* books. When my first son, Alex, was born, someone sent us a book of tips on how to be a mumsy and a popsy, and splashed across the front cover was a red-letter headline that said BOOK SMELLS LIKE BABY!!! I sniffed: Sure enough, the book reeked with the standard stench. It turns out the smell was concentrated in a stiff bright pink square of dense cardboard that was stuck loose between the pages in the middle of the book, kind of a super-duper scratch-and-sniff thing, but without the option of *not* scratching.

Well, if I could have convinced my publisher to be as olfactory (kind of like visionary, but different) as the one that published that book, the smell I got off Spencer's head would be rising from these pages now. Why? Because—as I decided right then, with the smell under my nose—that aroma was the unmistakable sensory message of (don't laugh) boyness. That is, human masculinity in its purest state.

Sure it was. And don't knock it: Most male animals deposit the unmistakable sensory message of *their* masculinity in a rather more richly scented form, compared to which the scalp gas of a wee laddie seems restrained and succinct. Spencer's aroma was definitely an animal scent too, but one made by a more refined gland. It was musky, but smart. It contained a mild wildness—the kind that might let someone want to utter a discreet howl at the moon once every couple of years or throw an unbuttered biscuit at a cousin now and then, but not the kind that would let you carry a bone around in your mouth and bury it in the backyard. The scent obviously claimed the right to be noticed, but it didn't shriek and beat its chest and wear a funny hat. It was all in there. And it smelled *good*.

When my wife came downstairs, I handed Spencer to her and was about to orate about my discovery. But before I could say a word, she lurched, held

Spence away from her face, and said, "Peee*yooo!* Let's go shampoo that head, Sweet Boy. You *stink!*"

And so she truly believed. The smell of her son's essence—indeed, the essence of all three of the major primo dudes among whom she has the privilege of inhaling—struck her as something to be immediately washed off. I protested, and defended the rich bouquet of exuded sebaceousness. She was as stunned at my enjoyment of it as I was at her finickiness. She said, "Look, I love the way he smells when he's—well, *clean.* But his head has been [grimace] *sweating.*"

And this made me realize: Boys don't mind giving off a pungent human aroma or smelling one. *Especially* if it involves a little perspiration. Girls would just as soon do neither.

It is important to note that my wife is absolutely not a fainthearted dip. She does not like The Baby Smell. She does not keep open jars of dead petals salted through the house "to freshen the air." She does not even wear perfume. Nine years with one son and one husband have taught her to grit her teeth and clench her nostrils a little now and then. But those nine years have not taught her to like what she smells, at least when the smell has ripened a bit through time and exertion.

Let me stipulate that being comfortable with a deep but decent aroma is not an act of self-adoration for the male. We would feel just as easy with a nat-

ural female pungency. At least, I *think* we would.
But since girls never seem to give off a pungent
natural aroma, even when they engage in sports,
we will never know. In the past twenty-five years I
have played lots of tennis and baseball and other
things with female athletes, and I have hung out
with them afterward, keenly alert, nose open. Nary
a niff.

If you know a great deal about natural science—
or if you watch dogs much, which amounts to the
same thing—you know that males have been given
the primary responsibility for emitting and savoring
odor in nature. It is the male who marks the boundaries of his family's territory with, er, scent, and it is
the male who goes around sniffing the boundaries
of the other guys' territories. Nature has endowed us
with glands and stuff that produce fragrance, and
noses that pick it up. Running around smelling glan-
dular secretions and such doesn't sound like the
greatest job in the world, but hey, somebody's got to
do it.

But—well, we seem to kind of even *like* it. You
never see a male dog approach a pile of another
dog's poop with a grim, weary air of resignation, as
if he is saying, "Oh, cripes, another bunch of turds.
I suppose I *have* to do my duty, but when, oh when,
will it all end?" No, the dog always darts to the
disgusting source of aroma and sucks in the phero-
mones eagerly, exhaustively. You have to yank *hard*

on the leash to get him away. And when seven or eight football players are slumping against their lockers in a tight, poorly ventilated little aisle after a long sweaty practice in uniforms that haven't been laundered since the previous week, and all they've managed to do is pull off their shoes and now they have to take a break and pant (pant!) for ten minutes before moving on to the next article of clothing, well, you never see them exactly hurry. It can get pretty cheesy in one of those little aisles. But everyone seems content—even a bit happy—to relax in the rich atmosphere.

That's the key, really: relaxing. We guys spend much of our lives being rushed to correct conditions that arise out of our natural tendencies. We know we produce a lot of unpleasant potential—through loudness, competitiveness, ribald humor, and roughness, any of which can turn into *anything*—and we hasten constantly to negate the consequences of ourselves. Our tendency to stink is one such source of unpleasantness. But it is one we can sometimes choose *not* to negate or rush away from, with no harm to anyone if circumstances are controlled (no females downwind).

Sometimes we enjoy abstract renderings of our bad tendencies; we watch boxing, for example. These abstractions are performed by other guys, however. A personal aroma is your own, and the aroma of the guy next to you, or the son under your nose, is *his* own, and putting up with each other's makes you feel kind of loose, and tolerant, and friendly.

Plus, sometimes, especially if it is a baby's head— well, it just smells pretty *good*. Considering what dogs have to put up with, I say there's nothing wrong with enjoying ourselves when we can.

Real Boys
Read Books

There is probably no more universally believed cliché about boys than this one: "Boys don't like to read." Walk into any school library, anywhere in the United States, and ask the librarian if she has trouble "getting" boys to read. Ask her if boys read only certain types of books (and ask if she could use more "*good* boy books"). Ask her if her favorite story of turning a resistant kid on to the unexpected joys of reading happens to be about a boy.

The answers will be "Yes!" absolutely every time. Now, I respect librarians as much as any group of educators, and as much as any group of people involved in making or reading literature, but they all have this misunderstanding about boys and they keep it rolling by acting as if it were true: "Boys don't like to read."

Certainly it's easy to see why they think so. For

one thing, most boys do not readily accept the books that librarians press upon them. When Ms. Peabody says, "Joey, you will love this story!" about a book with a dragon on the cover, Joey tends to squirm a little and adopt a gruff expression and decline the pleasure of checking out the book. Whereas if Ms. Peabody can even find a girl who hasn't *already* read the book, the girl snatches it and begins to devour it on the spot, probably exclaiming aloud with overt enthusiasm. When she finishes two days later, she brings the book back and asks for more, beaming, bouncing, talking, thanking Ms. Peabody left and right. Joey, meanwhile, is still working on the word METALLICA drawn in two colors of Bic pen ink on the cover of his notebook, a project he has elaborated for the past eleven days.

The contrast cannot be ignored. Girls set the standard boys do not reach; girls are good readers, boys are poor. Who can blame the librarians? Their Library Club has sixteen girls in it and only one boy, and he's the kind of bizarro who will spend an hour silently studying a map of Iceland for no reason, or two hours slowly reading through the unabridged dictionary. Otherwise it's all exuberant gals every day after school.

All I can say to these librarians is: There is a difference between embracing books in public and reading. Libraries are public; so are oral book reports. Reading is private. That means you never know who is doing it, alone. Whenever a librarian tells me she has used one of my books to "get" a nonreading boy to read a Good Book, I always say: How nice—but how can you be so sure he hasn't read the complete works of Mark Twain all by himself somewhere?

You wouldn't believe how much this idea shocks them. They absolutely cannot imagine the possibility. See, it is unimaginable to a girl (or a librarian who used to be a girl) that someone might read a book and (what a concept!) *deny* that he has done so. To think that a person might *sneak* to read and then pretend he *hasn't*—pretend even when other people around him are carrying on a snappy, fun conversation that openly demonstrates their erudition *in front of teachers*—well, this is too weird to believe. It's easier to believe such people don't like to read in the first place.

Ah, but nobody ever came upon a girl reading a book and said, "What the hell are you *doing*?" Nobody ever said to a girl, "Why don't you put that thing down and go outside and play some ball?" Nobody ever said, "I'm worried about you—always got your nose in a book." Nobody ever said, "Wimp!" or "Sissy!" or "Smart-ass show-off!" But these are exactly what most boys hear from fathers and brothers and other guys, most every time they let somebody catch them reading a book. It helps a little if the book has a sports figure on the cover, or a customized race car, or the victim of a werewolf attack. But even then some male is bound to say, "What's the matter with you, reading all the time?"

The message from men is simple: *Real boys don't read.*

Now, it may be that girls who do things thought ungirlish get told, "*Real* girls don't . . ." And it may be that it bothers them a lot. Certainly I am aware (and was aware growing up) of the fact that there are certain defined roles and behaviors considered appropriate for female children, just as there are for males.

But there are some differences in the magnitude of anguish felt by the boy being unboyish and the girl being ungirlish, especially these days. For example, a girl who wants to play football is not considered a weakling; if anything, she is criticized for being a bit too strong. But a boy who reads all the time is definitely *not* cited for having a surplus of strength. Boy or girl, would you rather have people consider you strange for being too strong or strange for being a wuss?

It is definitely great that society is beginning to realize that for girls to expand—and eventually to blast away—the boundaries of ridiculous roles requires only the encouragement of natural strengths and ambitions they already possess. But I fear it is going to be harder for society to do the similar thing for boys—to realize that allowing boys to expand means encouraging things heretofore seen as not only unboyish but weak, kinky, fancy-schmancy. Things such as "thinking" and "reading."

What men expect of "real" boys has not really changed much in two hundred years, maybe even two thousand. Boys are still supposed to be rugged, quiet, strong, independent (within reason), controlled (under the direction of some ultimate male authority), and decisive. They are not supposed to think too much, feel too much, or take any crap from anybody except perhaps their fathers. They are supposed to play sports. They are supposed to be interested in war and war toys and all kinds of heavy machinery, especially cars. The following things usually frowned upon in our society in general are okay (some are even essential) for boys to do:

- Be stubborn;
- Be angry;
- Fight;
- Get only middling grades;
- Be focused on the purely physical;
- Be focused on the purely immediate.

The following things usually supported by our society in general are *not* especially cool for boys to do:

- Be smart;
- Be artistic;
- Avoid fights;

- See both sides of issues;
- Fantasize;
- Be refined;
- Be content to be alone.

When you think about reading, it seems pretty clear which of these lists it matches, right? We—meaning especially we male adults—associate reading with all this iffy stuff: thinking, even daydreaming, engaging in aesthetic pleasures, engaging in subtlety . . . all sorts of effete no-nos. We are uncomfortable seeing a boy reading a book we don't know about, on a sunny day when he could be outside clanging elbows on a basketball court.

But why? It starts with trust versus control. Men don't really trust boys. We want to maintain a degree of control or at least surveillance that is impossible when a boy is reading *heaven knows what* and whirling it through his unpredictable little mind. But when he is running up and down a football field, we can *see* it all. We know what he's doing, even pretty much what he's *thinking*. Plus, he's *with* people. Men especially don't trust boys who are alone.

A deeper uneasiness comes from the question of intelligence and thought. Let's face it: Men don't feel they can admit that the intellect is okay to have and to use. So we get gruff, defensive writers such as Ernest Hemingway, a smart guy who spent his life trying to prove he'd *really* rather fish and fight bulls than do sissy stuff like think and write, but if he *has* to think and write, he'll do it in such a way that his prose is man's stuff: terse, tough, quiet, unambiguous, direct, focused on the physical, focused on the immediate, etc. Something like this:

> Jack walked down the path. The gun was cold in his hand. The dirt crunched against the heels of his boots. A Koolaboo bird screeched off to his left and he looked into the bush for its black pinions. Then it was night, and the path was finished, as finished as his marriage, and he was facing the mountain across the desert.
>
> The desert was big. The mountain was big. An elephant walked by and it was big too. "Not for long, old fellow," Jack said, shooting it between the seventh and eighth ribs.

In a man's book, if a guy shoots an elephant, he just shoots an elephant. He doesn't go mooning about the nature of life.

But this dismissal of the intellect, especially by a writer, is the rankest hypocrisy. Every writer, including Hemingway, knows very well that by setting up his little tersely depicted scenes in terms of the direct, the physical, and the unquestioned, he is encouraging his *readers* to think about the indirect, the nonphysical, the speculative. A writer knows that whatever he leaves out is what the reader will create for himself. And that what the reader creates for himself will prove more fascinating than anything he receives from the page. Want the reader to moon about the nature of life? Kill an elephant and don't let your *character* think about it; that will ensure that your *reader* will. But he'll fool himself, believing he is reading with his guts rather than with his smarts.

What men *really* feel funny accepting is something they correctly recognize in literature: technique. We like to pretend the use of technique is slightly dishonest, that it compensates for weaknesses no whole boy or man ought to have. We make a show of preferring behavior that demonstrates an unthinking sureness of action, an ideal simplicity we can equate with conviction. You got some land, you got some crop seeds, you plant them. You got some molten steel, you got some molds, you pour the stuff. You're carrying a gun, you see an elephant, you shoot the damn thing. Just *go out and do it*. Why make a fuss?

This, too, is hypocrisy. The farmer who doesn't study his land's contours, who doesn't practice with his tractor and disker, who doesn't investigate every variable of weather—the farmer, in short, who doesn't use technique—is going to lose his farm. Nobody just "goes out and does it" in farming. Ditto steelworking, ditto hunting. You tell me hunters just gruffly pick up guns and start bringing down wildfowl right and left? Forget it. That's like saying Michael Jordan just goes out and *plays,* as if he hasn't spent countless hours perfecting every single element of his crossover dribble, or his fake-the-dunk, scoop-the-shot reverse layup, or his no-look alley-oop pass.

Books, though, represent an entirely intellectual technique. Printed language has no substance: It takes mental manipulation to make it into a story. The writer manipulates it to *suggest* certain effects, and the reader manipulates it to *feel* these effects. This abstract handling is what adult males can't get happy with.

Is it clear by now that men not only feel indifferent to the possibility of their sons reading, but in fact feel a bit hostile about it? Oh, yes, things are changing a little. Yuppie dads buy their boys ten books a week, at least until the sixth grade; immigrant dads encourage their sons to crack the books constantly; boys in families that include illiterate grandparents are respected for mastering the magic of decoding print. But the mainstream view is: Don't read; instead, go play or work. Reading is for nerds and sissies.

All of which makes it hard for boys to do reading as a public thing. Boys want to be Real Boys, which means acting like the Real Men around them, and few of those men would be caught dead reading a book. (They don't count the sports page as reading. They should. Baseball cards and model-car directions and joke books, too.) Boys want to avoid anything that casts doubt upon their masculinity. They want to dissociate themselves from girls (who, as we have seen, have pretty much claimed libraries as their turf).

But—boys also want to read. They *love* to read, and not just sports books and car books and war books and werewolf books, either. When they *do* read these kinds of books, it is not just because they like sports or cars or war. It is because they like *books*.

And funnily enough, the main reason boys like to read is that they gravitate naturally toward activities that develop the strengths that will make them good men. Reading is an act of independence: You do it alone, and you are in charge. It is an act of liberty (liberty is good, right, men?): No one can tell you not to go back and reread the previous chapter twice, or not to skip ahead and read the ending early. It is an act of intelligence and imagination, which most men will squirmishly admit cannot be all bad. It is true that reading can be subversive—that is, it can allow boys to discover things men would rather hide from them, or encourage boys to think in ways men would prefer they didn't. But this relentless pursuit of discovery—finding things out for yourself, new things, your *own* things—is a big part of preparing for manhood.

Boys kind of know all along that *all* boyhood is sanctioned by this overall responsibility: Everything you do should have the purpose of turning you into a man. Can't we sanction books too, along with the fishing pole and the pet snake and the fistfight and the TD catch? Can't we sanction intelligence? If we are going to trust a twelve-year-old with a 20-gauge, can't we trust him with *To Kill a Mockingbird*? Let's practice saying it alone, first, aloud, before trying it out on the boys: "Reading is good. You don't have to join the library club. But reading books—well, it can help make you a good man."

Ten Things
You Cannot Expect Your
Mom to Come Close to
Understanding

1. That the paper cup full of a mixture of tooth-paste, chewed gum, and pine shavings from your gerbil cage is *a scientific experiment* that you have left for a week in the freezer *on purpose,* and that to throw it away as if it were nothing but a pair of old panty hose demonstrates *contempt for knowledge.*

2. That garments with holes in them often feel better than ones without.

3. That thirteen piles—okay, *loose* piles—of baseball cards on the floor of your room are not "a mess" that needs to be "cleaned up" but rather a *very carefully ordered* division of *extremely valuable* pieces of *entirely private* property.

4. That real food and dessert occupy different spaces in the physiology, so that *yes, you can too* be "full" of chicken-and-eggplant but still have room for a package of Twinkies.

5. That calling your best friend a "supersonic id-
    iotic brain-defective spaz" when he drops two
    passes in a row in the middle of a pickup foot-
    ball game is nothing but a sign of healthy com-
    petitive camaraderie.

6. That dirt is different from "germs."

7. That one doesn't so much "listen" to music as
    feel music, and one cannot feel much unless the
    music is sufficiently *loud*.

8. That you cannot "play" with your cousin who
    is a girl. You can sit in the same room with
    her, you can possibly even talk about a nice
    subject (though an argument is likely), you can
    eat junk food together. But neither of you
    can come anywhere near "playing" together,
    thank goodness.

9. That an obsession with a sport, during the sea-
    son of that sport, is not the sign of an aimless
    mind. That in baseball season, for example, it
    takes a lot of fervent intellectual effort to keep
    track of the batting averages, runs batted in,
    stolen bases, and home-run totals of your thirty
    favorite players and the won-lost records of the
    top three teams in all six divisions; to antici-
    pate the shifts in chemistry of teams involved
    in major trade rumors; to track the likely re-
    covery progress of five critical pitchers who
    have undergone surgery for a strained rotator
    cuff, a torn wrist ligament, a blocked artery in

the forearm, bone spurs along the anterior ulnar surface, and a hairline radius fracture that required magnesium pins to close. . . .

10. That you think she is actually pretty much okay, even though she doesn't understand squat.

Eight Reasons
Why Ice Hockey
Kicks Football's Tutu

know what you are saying: *"Ice hockey?* Better than *football?* Oh, sure. Next he'll be telling us math problems are more fun than rude mouth noises." Well, no, but I *will* assert that, for fans to watch and understand, the game of ice hockey is superior to the game of football at any level of competition, but most of all at the highest. In every area that should matter to a reasonable sports fan, the NHL pro pucksters outscore the NFL pigskinnies, and frankly, it's not even close.

This is difficult to admit, since I am a loyal American and football is red, white, and blue with stars. Hockey, a Canadian game, is *bleu, blanc, et rouge,* with ice. For a long time, even though four of the six pro teams were based in the United States, Canada had a lock on the sport, mostly because all the players and coaches were from north of the border. It is true that we Yanks are catching up pretty well now, faster than might have been expected, faster than we are catching up in, say, soccer, even though soccer is played by a lot more kids across the United States than hockey is. By the 1990s, about a third of the top players in the National Hockey League were Americans. Yesss! (Quite a few others are Russian and European. *Da!* It is our only truly international team sport.) But in the hearts and minds of American fans at large, hockey is still a curious, minor, clubby sport, on a level with, say, rugby, or lacrosse (which is also better than football, but let's save that for another book).

Let me state right now that I know I probably won't convince any of you to switch your mania from football to hockey. Hockey fans are crusaders, but we aren't fools. We know we live in the icy underground, and we know it is nearly impossible to get anyone to leave the spotlights and cheerleaders and TV cameras to join us down here. That's okay. Believe me, we know—how do I put this gently?—we know that, well, not everyone has what it *takes* to appreciate the subtleties and thrills of the world's fastest team sport. We are used to shaking our heads in amazement as you morons continue to throw away your leisure hours year after year on an endless series of televised games that show as much distinction one from the other, and as much unpredictability, as a tub full of eggs.

So go ahead—waste your life arguing about whether Troy Aikman will be better than Joe Montana, when in fact they may actually be the same person. But first, read this. If you're watching a game right now, you can probably finish the whole article in the space between two plays. Or wait for the next "break" of nine or ten commercials—it should be coming up any minute!

1. You Can Watch Football, but You Have to Follow Hockey

I realize that for a certain type of sports fan, it is no flaw for a game to be completely without mystery, spontaneity, or sustained action. This fan's idea of strategic insight is hollering "Gotta pass!" at the TV when his team faces third-and-sixteen. He thinks a coach is a wicked, risk-taking genius for daring to suppose that a 220-pound running back can probably travel two feet on fourth-and-inches. Wow! That's guts!

But some sports fans like to, well, *think*. And what makes them think is unpredictability. And what makes a sport unpredictable is constant action, in which unrelenting effort can suddenly produce an opportunity seized by a rush of teammates unified into a formation that could not have been foreseen just seconds before, whizzing into intuitive improvisation at incredible speed, making a new pattern for an old play, unleashing athleticism through creativity, skating, passing, and here's a *shot* . . .

Whew. Got a little carried away there—almost raised my butt off the chair! Of course, *your* butts are safe; you football fans don't have to worry about your game threatening your stolidity. You don't have to move your *head* to follow the action, much less your brain. In hockey, the transition from defense to offense happens every few seconds; in football, it's every ten or fifteen minutes. The play plods along in one direction, and then you get plenty of time to get ready for it to switch, and then it plods along in the opposite direction. You only have to be alert enough to notice if the guys with the ball are going from left to right on your TV screen, or from right to left. Quite a few of you can handle the challenge of this. About 150 million every Sunday, in fact. Kind of makes you feel special, doesn't it?

2. Football Is Slow, Slow, Slow—Even Slower Than Chess

It's true. In chess, the players have to make a move every three minutes. Often it's longer than that between second down and third down in a football game.

Seriously, watch ten minutes of football on TV. How many plays did you see? Probably about seven; fewer if you happened to hit one of those commercial "breaks" dictated to the league by network officials. Seven plays. What a thrill!

Now, switch to a hockey game (if you can find it). Watch for ten minutes. How many hockey plays did you see? *What?* You say you saw *two* plays? Oh—oh, yes, I see what you mean. You mean the whistle only blew once to stop play during the whole ten minutes. Yes, in football that *is* the way we decide what a play is: A play is what happens between whistles. But in hockey a play is a quick attempt to get your team the puck and turn the possession into a chance to score a goal at the other end of the ice. Plays involve and are defined by steals, passes, long end-to-end rushes by single players, body checks, more steals, more passes ... all without a whistle. Now, how many plays did you see? Fifty-six! Yes, that's more like it—that's hockey. (It's basketball, too. Many of hockey's good qualities can be found in hoops, but hoops doesn't need an essay to help it trash football. Besides, there's too much scoring in hoops, too many whistles, too much *height.* . . .)

Did you know that in a typical pro football game, there is eight times as much time *between* plays as there is *during* plays? An 8-to-1 ratio of dead time to action, during which: Six guys are running around making the wonderful "Number One!" gesture in the air because they just made a completely routine play, twelve guys are getting s·l·o·w·l·y up off the ground where frankly they look like they belong, four guys are running off the field because they play only on special second-and-eight plays heading east-west in the first quarter of night games, and the officials are putting their heads together and deciding nobody did anything wrong on the previous play.

Eight to one: You can time it yourself.

In ice hockey, the ratio is 6 to 1 the other way: six

minutes of action to one of dead time. And even during the dead time you get to watch guys doing cool little offhand skating moves without paying *any* attention to what their feet are cutting, moves that would take you five years to master, and even then you couldn't look so completely nonchalant about them.

As for speed within the play, consider: The only action in football that remotely approaches the surprise uprising and coalescent flow of a *common* offensive rush in hockey is an *especially wild* ninety-nine-yard kickoff or punt return. And you get, what, maybe four of those a season in the whole league? Yay!

3. No One in Hockey Makes All-Pro Because He Can "Execute"

Your superfine offensive football player today is the guy who doesn't mess up. The coach gives him a plan to follow for each play, a plan in which he has memorized his role exactly: "Take two steps to the left and block the outside linebacker, trying to hold him for two seconds," or "Run down eight yards, turn toward the sideline, look back, and catch the ball that should be arriving." If he completes his extremely limited tasks according to the plans devised by his coaches, in the sequence commanded by his coaches, then he is the ultimate hero to football fans: He is the pro who can "execute."

A player gets the highest praise in football for

sticking to the routine. The great receiver is the one who runs his routes crisply and without variation; the great quarterback is the one who delivers the ball to the end point of those routes with dependable sameness of elevation and speed. The great guard will always pull and run ahead of the back at the predictable pace, hitting the predictable defender. The running back is rather a wild man in this company, because sometimes he gets to do "open-field running," but most coaches would prefer a back who "follows his blockers" instead of free-lancing away from the path plotted for him. When these players do not allow themselves to get distracted by the pressures that give the play its context—the clock, the score, the fans, the seeming momentum established by recent plays—they show their finest quality.

Defensive players have a little more leeway to think for themselves and scramble to make a play, because the defensive role is at least partly a responsive one. The defender waits to see what his offensive opponent is going to do—or at least where he is going to line up. But then the plan of response clicks in: "Ah, they have three wideouts and a pro set, so we go into a strong-side zone shift with a man on the tight end and a weak-side safety blitz. All right, we're ready. Hut-hut-hut . . ."

But wait—we're not always ready. How many times have you seen a panicked linebacker call a frantic timeout because the offense lined up in an unforeseen way? "My *gosh*! They've split the tight end and put the running back in the *slot*, for crying out loud! And—and look at that tackle! *Whoa! Stop! We don't know what to do! Help, Coach!*"

Well, some of us say, you *do* know what to do: You tackle the guy who has the ball. What's the big deal? But football being what it is, the cool-headed captain who desperately stops the play is always right (and always much praised for his intelligence by the announcers). The reason he's right is that the actual action of the play hardly matters—once you know the formations, you practically know it all. They might as well not bother to hike the ball. I can foresee a day when the two teams break out of the huddles into formation and the officials study the alignment, blow their whistles before the snap, and award yardage or points based on the obvious discrepancy between one set and the other. What's scary is that the actual yardage or points that would have been gained in the *real* play would probably be close to what was awarded by decree—that's how incredibly predictable the whole thing is.

People praise football for this. They equate planning with intelligence, and conclude that football itself is a "smart" game. Allowing nearly complete domination through design, and *utter* domination by an endless array of twitchy geeky coaches (who are *so* smart they frequently burn out from the sheer amazing brainpower of it all; what the heck are they doing for sixteen hours a day that so exhausts the great mind?), the sport supposedly celebrates the perfect balance of intelligence and athleticism.

But wait. While it is true that the designing of a play is a function of *one* aspect of intelligence, and the repeatable execution of an eleventh part of that design is a function of *one* aspect of athletic ability, we cannot pretend this is all there is to do in sports. Intelligence is way, *way* bigger than what is exercised, however cleverly, in mere planning with *X*'s and *O*'s. And physical talent can express itself in a zillion ways, not just through the cool repetition of the take-seven-steps-and-turn sorts of regimens, however demanding those tasks are.

Personally, I like to see the *players* think—not just the coaches—and I like to see them have to do so in the midst of constant, shifting challenges. This, too, is a way of being smart, and a game that requires such a use of wits can be called a "smart" game as easily as football can. Quickness and flexibility are qualities of intelligence to be prized as highly as planning.

A great football coach may be a genius of anticipation. But a great hockey player is a genius of improvisation. One big difference between the two is initiative. Hockey players make up their own minds on the spot about what to do. The coaches put them on the ice and trust them to be smart and opportunistic and tough. In other words, they treat them like *men*. A football coach, on the other hand, leaves his players no initiative; he makes *all* the decisions. It's almost as if he doesn't trust them, isn't it? "I can't let you boys play this important game on your own—it's simply too big for you. Let Daddy tell you exactly what to do, and we'll all get along fine." Yes, Daddy. How many steps do I take on this play?

Another big distinction between anticipation and improvisation is creativity. It's the difference between reciting a poem somebody else wrote and writing your own; between being a DJ and being a composer. Football is so devoid of this quality that when a little tiny bit of creativity pops up in a game, everyone goes bananas to glorify it. Remember the amazement we bestowed on John Elway during the half-season in which he was "allowed" by Dan Reeves to "call his own (selection of the coaches' array of preset) plays"? Jeez, we acted as if he were Mozart or something. Same with Jim Kelly and all his audibles. And if Jerry Rice grabs a short pass and shakes his defender and bops down the field for twenty-eight yards thanks to a couple of very fine hip fakes and the good sense to use two blocks delivered by 280-pound guys in front of him, we speak as if he had just invented water. Just imagine: He caught the ball, saw that he could gain some more yards, and figured out a way to run for five more seconds! What a wild presence! Such initiative! He's a go-to guy, ain't he?

In the game of football Jerry Rice is indeed a superb player. But the things he manages to do a couple of times per game are things a decent forward does twenty times a game in hockey. A *decent* forward, not an all-star. As for the creativity of calling plays—well, a good center iceman improvises as many plays as Elway calls, but does it on the spot, in a couple of seconds, *and* brings his teammates into his idea sheerly through a kind of very fast, very subtle communication composed of athletic moves and will. When you watch a *great* center—and in the '90s we have at least eight Hall of Fame centers playing every night—when you watch one of these guys spot a possibility on the ice and turn it into a collaborative attack in the space of three seconds while everyone is whizzing along at twenty-five miles per hour, and it works as if it had been diagramed *but it wasn't*, then you can talk about initiative and authority.

Unanticipated formations are coming at the hockey player from new angles every ten seconds, and he knows this when he steps on the ice. He's on his own; there is no *"Timeout! Help, Coach!"* You are always moving, so the vectors are always opening up new problems and chances, within which you had better be ready to play fast. If a guy has the puck and he is bearing down on you, you need to instantly compute his speed and angle against your own, and the position of teammates (his and yours) in front of and behind him and the location of the goal and the blue line, and then—taking all of this into account—you need to get the dang puck.

Well, yes. In terms of momentary strategy, it really

is that simple: *Get the dang puck*. But while a defensive football player would be almost helpless if you
just said *"Tackle the man with the ball"* and let the
other guys hike it, and while his defense would get
scored upon time after time, a hockey player can
pretty much make do with this minimal direction.
That's why a lot of hockey games are 3–2 instead of
56–10.

4. Football Has No Goalies

All right, here we go. It's third-and-two at the Red-
skin 28. Rypien takes the snap, fakes a handoff to
Byner, rolls left and looks upfield. The linebackers
bought the play-action fake and the safeties went for
Art Monk and Desmond Howard and *oh my gosh*
Ricky Sanders is in single coverage and he's got his
cornerback beat and Rip flips him a nice pass. Sanders gathers it in at the 40 in full stride, then just as
one safety scrambles up, Ricky stutter-steps and cuts
back inside, zipping past the falling defender, and
then he jukes past the second safety and stiff-arms a
pursuing linebacker and then it's a footrace against
the last linebacker, and, yes, it's obvious, Ricky is
pulling away, *oh yes* he's got the speed, he's at the 30,
the 25, the 20, he's going to *score* oh *yesss* . . . But just
as he crosses the 5-yard-line a chunky little man
holding a long padded club runs up and swats him
in the knees and Ricky goes down at the 2. Whoa!
The crowd roars. *What a save* . . .

Face it. Wouldn't football be more interesting if,

for the whole game, there was one wild little guy who prowled the goal line and had the job of spiking anyone who tried to get across after breaking free of the rest of the defense? Give the guy a couple extra pieces of equipment—a big padded stick, maybe, and a huge net for snagging passes—but restrict him to playing inside the 5. Can you dig it? What a nutty idea!

Far too nutty, of course, for football, which is the most conservative game in the history of the world, so stodgy it makes track and field seem wildly innovative. And far too restrictive of the offense all fans love. But—just for a second—can't you sense that such a defender would add a fascinating new challenge to the offense? As it stands now, if a wideout is faster than a cornerback and he gets the ball in a race down the sideline, speed alone will let him score. If a running back scoots through a hole in the line and can outrun the linebackers, he can get a quick six.

Should mere speed—not so much a skill as a gift—be so heavily rewarded?

It isn't in hockey, even though being a fast skater requires a lot more athletic skill than simply being a fast runner. Speed is a big advantage, but it is not decisive. The hockey player who steals the puck from an opponent, twirls away from him in a spin-o-rama move, accelerates away from three pursuers, fakes the final defender out by slipping the puck between his skates and racing around to pick it up behind him, then blazes in on goal in a noble burst of speed—*still* has to sneak the puck past a preternaturally quick and focused goaltender, who is ready and waiting for his tricks, armed with a big stick, a huge catching glove, and leg pads like small sofas. And who will stop about nine out of every ten shots.

To some people this sounds like an unnecessary negation of offensive effort, an enforced futility. All we can say is that those are the breaks: Hockey is founded on the premise that it should be very difficult to score.

What does it do for the game, when you make it so hard to score? Well, it makes the players work hard at every moment, because they know they cannot count on a three-run homer or a seventy-seven-yard bomb to break the game open. You scramble, press, scramble, press, scramble, press, and eventually one of those shots avoids the flailing stick or the fleet glove and goes into the net. The rarity of the chance makes the goal really mean something.

Goalies can be partial equalizers between teams of different quality: A hot goalie can keep his less adroit teammates in a game against better players, while a cold goalie can allow even the best team to slip against weaker competition. Usually, the bad team with the great goalie doesn't win a lot over the long haul, and the great team doesn't lose all the time either. But game by game, goaltending can make a critical difference, and this makes things even more interesting in a league of twenty-odd teams.

As far as team dynamics go, the figure of the hockey goalie has no counterpart in football. The goalie is something between a mascot—a wild animal mascot—and a starting pitcher. When announcers on the radio mention other games going on around the league, they always mention the goalies (". . . and Chicago is at Vancouver, Belfour against McLean . . .") just as a baseball announcer will mention pitchers (". . . Boston at Baltimore, Clemens against Mussina . . ."), because identifying the goalies tells you a great deal about what the game is probably going to be like.

The other guys on the team don't begrudge the goalie this extra fame, however; they figure he deserves it. After all, he is crazy (for *trying* to get in the way of a hard-rubber disk coming at him at one hundred miles per hour) and stupefyingly brave. Hockey players, like all other athletes, would just as soon forgo all bodily pain—but goalies, by definition, welcome it, for the good of their team. Often, the goalie has to stop the puck because a teammate has messed up a defensive task, giving the opponent what *would* have been a sure goal if it weren't for the goalie's guts and athleticism. This kind of thing inspires a lot of respect. It also inspires immediate gratitude and determination. Time and time again, a breathtaking save is followed immediately by an equally breathtaking rush down the ice and a fabulous goal at the other end. This happens so often it is practically a cliché: Defender messes up, goalie makes great save, teammates driven by gratitude and adrenaline whiz down and score. This is emotion. This is mutual dependence and inspiration. This is the world's most thrilling team sport.

5. Woody Hayes Was Never the World's Greatest Hockey Coach

He did enjoy that position in the world of football, however. His Ohio State teams churned their way through the Big Ten year after year for about nine decades, like a road grader grinding it out from Columbus to Pasadena at a steady twenty miles per hour. Woody's teams were famous for their single offensive play, an off-tackle run. It was called "Student Body Left," because all the players flooded to one side and the running back lugged the ball in their wake. The great phrase that was used to describe Woody-ball was "Three yards, and a cloud of dust." Woody once made the profound observation that if you could simply gain three yards every play and stop the other team from scoring just one time, you would win every game. Whoopee! Are we having fun yet?

On the few occasions when today's football manages to be graceful and a weentsy bit unpredictable and loosened up, it is because the offense is throwing the ball. Woody, however, eschewed the pass, and his comment about it is widely held to be as wise as the Golden Rule: "Only three things can happen on a pass play, and two of them are bad." So, instead of *inviting disaster,* let's *play it safe* and go Student

Body Left. If football had not had the benefit of its one tactically innovative coaching genius—Don Coryell, who flat believed in putting the ball *up*—we would all be watching clouds of dust for six or nine hours on Sunday.

Or, rather, *you* would. Me, I'll be watching people whirl around the ice in search of sudden brilliance. In hockey it is simply impossible to play it safe. Certainly there are conservative teams, and times in a game when you want to play conservatively (the third period when you have a two-goal lead, for instance). But even at its most conservative, the game of hockey contains vastly more wild risk and unpredictability than football, because the action never stops flowing. Hockey has coaches too, of course, and even game plans and position roles. But except for the slowed-down times when one team is penalized and the other has a one-man advantage for a few minutes, there is no such thing as executing an offensive play with certainty. And you have to keep playing offense, *crazy* offense, because it isn't possible to run off tackle and eat up the clock on a sustained drive in hockey.

Woody Hayes did not finish his career as the world's most boring athletic theorist, however. He finally cracked, and did something pretty interesting. In a big, nationally televised bowl game, his team's heroic last-minute drive toward a come-from-behind victory was thwarted when an opposing player intercepted an Ohio State pass (*see* what happens?). The kid who intercepted sidestepped a tackle and broke down the sideline, completely in the clear for the killing touchdown. But Woody wouldn't have it. He charged out onto the field, trailing wires from his headset, still carrying his clipboard, and he viciously tackled the absolutely perplexed kid ("Coach Hayes? *Coach? Uuumph!* . . .").

That was it—Woody was forced to retire, just when he was showing signs of innovation. See how football authorities react to creative ideas?

6.   Fighting Is Better Than Woofing

There used to be a "joke" that went like this: "Last night I went to the fights and a hockey game broke out." Har har har! This somehow passed for wit, but only among people who had never been near a hockey game in their lives. People who don't watch hockey "know" one thing about it: Those big mean toothless men have fistfights! This senseless violence has no place in our society's entertainments! (So let's switch channels away from this nasty game and let Junior watch cartoons or a cop show, where he will see an average of 9.5 violent deaths—*deaths!*—per hour.)

I don't like fights in hockey games. Partly it's because they are lousy fights: two guys slipping around on ice skates for thirty seconds, grabbing each other's jersey and occasionally glancing a blow off the top of each other's fiberglass helmet. As soon as one guy starts to land any real punches, the officials break it up, and the combatants leave the ice, often for the rest of the game. Hockey fights can rarely be classified as "violence" under even the broadest, churchy definition of the term. What they are is b·o·r·i·n·g. Also, they provide a role and a job for guys who have no business in professional sports, because they are not skilled athletes so much as thugs who can beef around on skates.

Happily, the NHL has recently taken some good steps to get rid of fighting, by telling the referees to call stiffer penalties on the teams of the players who start them. (The league is also trying to cut down on hockey's real violence, the constant macho crunching along the boards and behind the play that is meaner and more dangerous than any fight.) In 1992–93, the first year under the new rules, there was about one fight per five games—none of which got out of control and flared into one of those big brawls that everyone sees on the news. Even in the past, there were only one or two superfights per year in the whole league schedule, over one thousand six hundred games. There have always been very few fights in the play-offs. (But, unfortunately, in the 1993 play-offs the refs did revert to condoning non-fight thuggery on the ice.)

So, thirty or forty seconds—we'll even say a full minute—of ineffectual scuffling in five hours of pure action. Barbaric! Let's switch to this exciting football game instead, okay?

Okay! Look, there's a huddle. The offense is waiting for the play to come in from the coach on the sidelines, who is busy listening to information relayed from the observers way up in a booth in the stands. Hmm, it's taking a while—twenty-six seconds, in fact. But now the play is called, and the guys are coming up to the line of scrimmage and settling into formation (eight more seconds). The quarterback is hollering signals (five seconds). There's the hike! Barry Foster is getting a handoff and running into the line, where he is knocked down by a defensive tackle for the Eagles. That took just under three seconds, but boy, oh boy, they were some *great* seconds! And now the defensive tackle is jumping up and beating his chest and shaking his index finger in Foster's face (five seconds). Now he's stomping around swinging his fist in the air (six seconds), and some of his teammates are jumping up and down and slapping him on the helmet (eight more seconds). Gosh, what great camera work—we're not missing *any* of this thrilling football action! And now the screen is flashing a still photograph of the defensive tackle. He's some player, huh? Imagine—he's only twenty-five years old, weighs just 285 pounds, gets paid $1.6 million a year to tackle running backs who come near him, and—wow, get ready—*he just tackled a running back who came near him!* It's awesome. Who can blame him for celebrating his personal accomplishment for twenty or thirty seconds? This is one gritty, fascinating sport!

Fascinating? Watching guys go into fits of onanism for executing a few numbingly elementary and brief tasks? Give me a break! This is a true story, by the way, and you can verify it yourself with a stop-watch, on any series of downs in any NFL game, anytime. The ratio of on-camera woofing to action is better than 4 to 1. Four times as much prancing, strutting, chest puffing, air punching, taunting, hip gyrating as there is running or throwing or catching or tackling.

How's this for a joke: "Last Sunday I went to watch a bunch of overprivileged young men shamelessly exult in themselves in front of television cameras, and a football game broke out!"

I can hear a lot of protests already out there, claiming that the celebrations are essential rites of self-expression common to all-male warrior societies, or that the guys are just unleashing spontaneous brio, or that it's a boys-will-be-boys thing. Well, I go to peewee football games and I can testify that *real* boys don't do this trash. They act like *real* men, making plays, enjoying the action, staying modest and teamish. As for spontaneous brio—well, there is nothing spontaneous about most woofing. It's practically a scripted performance, as some players admit: Last year I read an interview with an NFL wideout who said he and his colleagues spend a lot of time in front of the mirror polishing their scoring dances. "Sorry, Coach, can't make it right now—got this little crossover step with a hip shake to get down. . . ."

There's a little more to the self-expression excuse. As we have seen, it is true that football allows very little opportunity for players to do something creative. Also, it calls itself a team sport, but because each play is broken down into eleven individually executed parts, the feeling of joining your buddies to make something spontaneously happen is hard to come by. This leaves a player feeling that he has a very limited range of pretty impersonal functions. And because football players grow up believing they are fabulous individual stars, this dull anonymity chafes. So every chance a star-type guy gets to flash himself above the muddle, he jumps up and down and says, "Watch *me*! Here I am! *Me! The real me!*" Of course, he isn't a warrior, and his team is not a society. He is a performer, sharing the stage with eleventy other performers, all waiting for their chance to show off for the cameras.

The cameras are important. Football is not so much a game anymore as a TV show (the primary purpose of which is to set up the beer, car, sneaker ads, which actually contain more action than the game). Pro football is designed and produced for TV, just like any other program. The NFL season is a regular prime-time series, and the players act a lot more like TV stars than athletes. Why not? Television is where their celebrity really comes from, and their money.

Alas for poor hockey. Not ready for prime time— the game cannot be neatly packaged, predicted, canned. The players can't consider themselves media stars. So they are all kind of dorky and rough hewn, generally camera shy, giving very simple interviews while looking at the locker room floor. As for showing off individually during the game—I'm afraid it's seen as not being exactly, well, very *manly*. Or very well deserved: The shooter who nets the goal usually profited from the hard work of a couple of teammates who got the puck to him in good position to score. (That's why an assist counts the same as a goal in the tabulation of individual scoring stats.) Sure, after a goal the guys all raise both arms in the air for maybe four seconds. This happens, on the average, six times a game, counting both teams.

It is *only* a goal that is celebrated in even this modest fashion, however. After a good play equivalent to a tackle or a nice catch or a tipped pass in football, the hockey player cannot take twenty seconds to juke and howl, for the simple reason that the game races on around him. You steal the puck, you better look for someone to pass it to and follow the rush and be ready to back up and play D when the shot is turned away and the other guys grab the rebound and bear down on you. If you're dancing, the man you are supposed to cover is going to burn your teammates.

Perhaps being too fast keeps a game a sport. It certainly keeps it from becoming a TV show.

7. The Last Two Minutes of a Hockey Game Take Two Minutes

I suppose there is a kind of tension to be teased out by all of the clock-stopping shenanigans that make the last two minutes of a football game take as long as twenty minutes to play. But it's a phony kind of suspense, without any relation to the human sensibility. Time is supposed to be the problem here, but the fan's sense of time passing relentlessly is exactly what football's endgame destroys.

If your hockey team is behind by a goal two minutes from the end, your frantic suspense about whether or not they'll score in time is *driven* by your sense of those two minutes flying away. Nobody's stopping the clock, and the seconds are ticking inside you just as they are on the ice. The players down there are pressing themselves with the same increasingly desperate urgency *you* feel as the end approaches fast. They have no recourse to stretch-it-out stratagems like running out of bounds or downing a pass. They have to do the job right now, in real time. Somehow, that makes it seem a lot more like a real challenge.

8. Hockey Is Not Like Life

It is often said, "Football is like war." This is incredibly ridiculous, trying to filch the seriousness of purpose and desperation of commitment needed for humanity's greatest strategic horror and apply them to a simple, rather silly game. Calling the line of scrimmage "the trenches" and all that sort of over-blown battle-allegory stuff is contemptible.

Football is, however, exactly like a very common kind of modern life. And I can certainly see why this makes it appealing to a certain kind of sports fan. With its emphasis on planning instead of surprise, its division of labor, and—most of all—its mechanical progress through increments, football is exactly like an idealized workday, or school day, or work-week, or school year, or career. The working man who watches his football team grinding its way, yard by yard and first down by first down, to the goal line cannot fail to sense a confirmation of the soundness of his own efforts. Life, after all, goes in increments: We work toward the next "first-down marker"—a report card, a completed project, a new level of quarterly sales, a promotion, a new car, a third child—and take a rest, and then set our sights on the next stage, confident that if we just keep our head down and stick to the task we have been given, we will one day get to pay dirt as a matter of steady endurance. Three yards and a cloud of dust, and eventually you arrive.

Although a boy is not a working man, there is in most boys a premonition of this life, whether it comes from genes, culturally induced roles, school routine, or imitation of a working father. Football appeals to that premonitory sense, I think; it is practically a cultural model of The Regular Life.

Hockey, on the other hand, is nothing like life at all—unless maybe it is life on Neptune. The players use curved sticks to swat at a rubber biscuit and whip it into a little net guarded by a strange, padded man, in a constant flow of action each step of which is an attempt to make use of the utter surprise of the previous moment. And, oh yes, they do it all on *ice*.

Do you like your sports to take you somewhere new and strange? Or do you like your sports to remind you of your daily routine? Perhaps this is what separates the football fan from the hockey fan, at heart. In life, we have to learn to tolerate exactly the things a football fan must bear every week: a pace that can seem slow, dull, and all too predictable; the specialization of roles that destroys a sense of wholeness; the artificial exaggeration that makes ordinary things appear spectacular; encounters with braggy jerks; television and all of its warpo effects. Some people see such things as a curse of modern life. Almost all of us have adjusted to them. Football fans have gone one step further, and found a way of celebrating them. To whatever degree this allows them to celebrate their own lives, I applaud it, in all sincerity.

But I'll keep heading to the Neptunian underground. It's *cool* down here.

Victory

When the two-time defending-champion Duke University basketball team was eliminated from the 1993 NCAA tournament, Coach Mike Krzyzewski held a press conference. It was one of those touching ones. Coach K (sorry, you'll get me to spell that name only once), with obvious sincerity, wept while proclaiming what a privilege it had been for him to coach the two seniors who had just played their final game under him. He let fly with a good half-dozen of our most time-honored sports clichés, all of them deeply heartfelt. (That's the worst thing about clichés, isn't it? They are often fairly accurate. Whether this is because they are great expressions of natural law, or because we tend to train our emotions to fit the most obvious, accepted forms is not entirely clear. Never will be.)

Coach K's final comment was actually pretty interesting, and will come as a surprise to most boys. After all the usual these-are-the-finest-young-people-in-the-world stuff and the they-gave-me-110-percent-every-time business, he tried to put the whole values thing in perspective. "People think winning is important," he said, fighting the tears. "But winning ... [sob, gulp] ... winning doesn't mean a damn thing."

Cut to tearful, wildly applauding audience. Yes! Winning means nothing! Take *that,* all you hyper-competitive men and boys! This is apparently what Americans want to hear now. Who cares about blunt facts like "won" or "lost" in something as rich in nuance and personality as a game? Heck, if coaches keep up this kind of thing for a few more years, the people in America who have been critical of sports mania since Vince Lombardi said, "Winning isn't the *main* thing. Winning is the *only* thing," won't have anything left to be scared of. And the rest of us, the people who play and follow sports with sometimes shamefaced avidity, can reform, so we won't have to go on feeling guilty all the time—guilty because now, gee, we kind of *do* want, well, to, you know, *win.*

The eagerness with which many people embrace Coach K's teary sentiment is nothing but a sign of how the style of masculinity has changed in our culture. Big-time sports has always been simply a reflection of how we wanted to view men. When everyone wanted to think of men as grim hard-ass unflinching tough-guy warriors, then "winning was the only thing." (What good did it do the Romans to finish second to the Visigoths?) Nowadays everyone wants to think of men as sensitive repentant deep-feeling human beings determined not to offend anyone with their crude tendency to overpower, so "winning means nothing." (We should apologize to the Iraqis.) What we demand of men, we of course demand of boys—only faster, with more purity. Snap to it! Get sensitive! Don't torture that frog! Don't win that game! Don't try to finish dinner faster than your brother, or get on the school bus first!

The truth is, of course, that manhood, like womanhood, cannot be defined by this style or that; men *are* warriors sometimes, and hard-ass too, but they are also sensitive touchy-feely types. A guy can drop bombs on Baghdad one moment and block-print a sweet letter home to his four-year-old daughter the next, weeping as sincerely as Coach K. As always, *any* attempt to limit a human being to a prescribed formula of anticipated behavior is ridiculous.

So switching clichés from Mean Guy to Kind Fellow doesn't really tell us much about anything but style. In fact, switching clichés actually *obscures* what should be a matter of great interest and concern: the whole notion of competition for victory.

Saying that winning means nothing is clearly false—just as it was false to say winning meant everything. The fact is, winning means *something*. For one thing, it means people line up to hear you talk about how little it means. After all, if Duke's record for the past two seasons had been 7–23 and 8–21, then who would have cared about Coach K's tender feelings? Which newspapers and TV stations would have sent reporters to cover the sentimental ramblings of a loser? I am certain there are a couple hundred coaches out there who wish they could express their gratitude to seniors moving on, who feel exactly as Coach K does, with the same sincerity. How come we haven't heard *their* comments rebroadcast over and over on TV and radio? Could it have anything to do with the fact that Duke won the previous two big ones?

I do not for an instant question the absolute honesty and profundity of Coach K's feelings about winning. I think that what he meant at that moment was this: "I like these fellows. I have seen them grow up, from boys to men, while they happened to be playing basketball for me. I recognize that they would have grown up even if they had not been playing basketball, so I am grateful to have been close to them during the process of personal development. They are wonderful young men *not* because they are champions; the game and its prizes seem small and superficial compared to the mysterious beauty of how humans come into themselves." All true.

But—pardon me for pointing this out—there is something a little disingenuous about a superwinner putting down winning. No one can deny that it's easier to say "Winning means nothing" with two consecutive national titles in your pocket than it is to say it if you've just gone 7–23 and missed the tournament for the nineteenth straight year. It's easier for a rich man to say, "You know, money really isn't where it's at" than it is for a poor man. Most poor men would say, "Hey, just give me the dough and let me discover the meaninglessness for myself." One cannot help but ask: Did Coach K feel winning didn't amount to much three years before, when UNLV humiliated Duke in the championship game by the biggest margin ever?

Actually, he probably did. He probably sat there in the locker room and looked around at his seniors and said, "You know, we just got killed, but I don't feel like a failure. These are some great kids we got here." But when somebody has just eaten your lunch, you can't announce you weren't hungry anyway without sounding pretty weak. Besides, if someone had offered Coach K victory at that moment instead of defeat, I'm sure he would have taken it.

And if you fast-forward to Duke's first month of practice next fall, and Coach K finds three of his very talented recruits feel indifferent about winning—they lack that famous killer instinct, they just like to play well and enjoy the opportunity to grow as humans—do you think for an instant that he is going to sit back and let them fulfill their potential for niceness, let them say, "You know, Mike, I really respect the program at Chapel Hill and I find it hard to hate Dean Smith!"? Forget it! He's going to get in their faces until they want to rip throats every time they see the word *Carolina*. Or *Wake Forest*, or *Virginia*. You don't win back-to-back NCAA titles by bringing up young men to eschew victory. We'll just see if Coach K's repudiation stays in the realm of principle or makes it onto the court. Personally, I think we'll see him in the Final Four again pretty soon, efficiently pursuing the utter athletic destruction of every young man in a different-colored shirt who gets in his way.

And he should do so! Let's face it: *We want to win!* Every time! The whole idea of a game—a contest— is for someone to emerge victorious. Let us say so! Let's not deny it. As I said above, I don't think Nice Mike really meant to say that winning means nothing. I think he meant that even if you win, there are other things you discover that mean more than simple victory.

So, okay. Fine. We can all get next to that; we like to see our victors show a deeper side, show some "character," which means, usually, some sober, mannerly appreciation of the bigger things in life. We would all have hoped that if Michigan had defeated North Carolina in the 1993 championship game, the Michigan players, notorious at the time for their taunting during games, would *not* have come on camera and waggled their hips and said, "Hooooeeee! Carolina sucks! We whupped their sorry *tails!* You see that reverse slam I stuck in Eric Montross's *face?* Man, we are the *best,* they are the *rest,* we *beat,* we *beat,* we *beat!*" Yet it might have been hypocritical of them to say anything *but* that, and hypocritical of *us* to expect them to do the classic good-sport bit—

smile a shy smile and say, "Well, we were fortunate enough to come away with the win, but we have a lot of respect for Carolina; they played a heck of a game . . ." Hey! We put the camera on athletes because we want to see them get desperate, we want to see them spill the last drop of blood in the effort to rally against the horror of defeat. Why should we pretend it is otherwise?

Instead of denying the value of victory, we need to look carefully at how we can integrate the yen for winning into the whole scheme of good values. Because it is deep in there already, down in the elemental voodoo of our natural ambitions, desires, inspirations. Subtract every game society has ever created, and we'll invent new ones. Put out sweetsy books (there were quite a few circa 1969) on noncompetitive children's games in which "every player is a winner!!!" and kids will immediately twist the rules around so that somebody gets to beat, somebody gets defeat.

Boys, especially, will do so. Given any opportunity, boys will declare a contest and strain to win it. My son Alex and I spend three or four evenings a week playing street hockey together on a blacktop behind a nearby school. It never occurred to us to play against each other, or at least it never occurred to *me;* instead, we practice long, fast breakaways with complex skating and passing schemes. When the shooter scores, we both raise our arms and slap gloves and all that: "Nice shot!" "Well, nice *pass!*" "Thanks!" "You're welcome!"

Cooperation! Congeniality! Every player a winner!!! Well, one night another kid from the neighborhood, a frequent playmate of Alex's, came with us on his skates. Oh boy, I thought—now we'll *really* have some fun, intertwining three skaters instead of two, passing from both wings, dropping passes for the trailer, and so on. Yippee! But the first time I took the puck and started down one wing with Alex on the other, this kid set up as a defender and stole the puck off me. I was shocked—naked antagonism! Meanwhile, he had turned and skated for the net, and Alex had checked *him* and stolen the puck back. Did my son then look for ol' Dad and sling me a nifty, chummy pass? No; he snapped a wrist shot through the other kid's legs and said "Yessss!" in his face, and they both laughed and spent the next hour trying to beat each other to bits in one-on-one, around-the-world, slap-shot accuracy tests, skating time trials . . . Me, I kind of skated around by myself, pushing a pebble with my stick and pretending to pass to Wayne Gretzky. When we left, Alex—grinning, flushed, bleeding from a new cut on his chin—said, "Now, *that* was fun!"

Is this wrong in boys? Of course not. Yet the competitive urge is one of the things males, especially boys, are most universally criticized for. Certainly it is one of the features of boys that makes them pains in the neck for teachers, parents, siblings ... everyone but coaches, in fact. You can't ask a group of boys to do anything without having them immediately turn it into a contest, often a pretty fierce one. ("Joey, can you and Sam and Andre straighten the desks? Boys, slow down! Sam, you kicked that desk in front of Andre! Joey, help Sam up! Boys! It's just *desks,* for God's sake! Boys ...") Every parent of a boy has to spend many pained hours convincing him that, no, you did not just "lose" because your friend got a better grade on a spelling test than you did (or got a bicycle a weekend earlier, or pulled a Frank Thomas insert worth twelve dollars from a Fleer Ultra pack while you got only a Cal Ripken worth ten dollars, etc., etc., etc.). The parent tries to say: It wasn't a contest! Each of you was in it for yourself! There's no reason to compare and compete! Why risk losing when you don't have to?

Ah, but there is always a contest, and we ought to admit it—I don't mean only *confess* it, I mean literally *admit* it, admit competitiveness to the brotherhood of natural emotions that simply must be accepted at full value. A few years ago, the touchy-feely movement received a huge boost when a research project showed that the top executives of the top businesses in America were actually not competitive types: They were "self-actualizers." Instead of fretting about who was gaining on them and whom they were beating, they simply focused on fulfilling themselves without reference to others, and *voilà!* they wound up on top.

So everybody said: See? The winners never even entered the race! Competition is unnatural and does not lead to success!

I think the study sounds great, but the conclusion is bogus. It's not that the top execs weren't competing; it's just that they figured out that concentrating on making yourself a hotshot is the best way to win. I mean, sure, Carl Lewis doesn't keep turning his head the whole one hundred meters to check out how the guys in the other lanes are doing. But just because he looks straight ahead and keeps his mind on his own stride doesn't mean he ain't *racing*!

We're all aware of the drawbacks of being too competitive about too many things—the artificial enmity, the temper, the resentment, the trees instead of the forest, the cheapness of the thrill, and so on. Are we aware of the benefits? Isn't competitiveness a spur to determination? Sometimes it is a ridiculous, painful spur, but, come on . . .

Again, perhaps our problem with facing the fact that winning *does* mean something comes from our inability to integrate it into our system of nice values. If we cannot even integrate it into the world of *sports*—if we have to say it means either "everything" or "nothing"—where you would think competitiveness was part of the whole idea, then what hope is there?

Well, it so happens the best person I've seen at handling victory and values is a college basketball coach. No, it isn't Coach K with his sincere, tearful homilies and his completely charming persona. Neither is it John Thompson, with his fierce commitment to big-picture social justice and responsibility. No, the main values man is, in fact, the coach who to most people represents the complete opposite: To these critics, he is the ugliest, foulest-tempered, baddest-behaving, winning-orientedest dude in the NCAA. I refer, of course, to Bobby Knight of Indiana.

I spent six years at the University of Iowa, and I saw a lot of Indiana's Big Ten and NCAA tourney games, year after year. And I guess that for every one chair he ever kicked, Bobby Knight taught twenty young guys some difficult lessons about how to pursue the goals of sport—including victory—*within* the more serious pursuit of manhood.

He did not always look good doing it; neither did his teams or their records. I recall one game, in which Indiana came to Iowa City for a very important nationally televised game. Indiana was the defending national champion; both teams were ranked in the Top Ten in the country; both were undefeated in the Big Ten. *Huge* game. In the first few minutes, things were close; in fact, Indiana took the lead. But Bobby Knight did not like the way his starters were playing. They weren't hustling, and they were jawing too much at the Iowa players. Acting too much like, well, winners. So he took them out, and put in five freshmen.

This is five minutes or so into the game, now. No big deal. The starters sat down, grinned sheepishly,

toweled off, shrugged and nodded. Yep, I guess ol'
Coach is right. I guess we see we weren't playing
right. I guess we'll let him make his point, and then
we'll get back in there and take it out on those
Hawkeyes! Right, Coach? Yes? Gee, Coach, the scrubs
in there, they've given up the lead and now Iowa is
kind of taking over. Isn't it about time for us to go
back in? Coach?

Well, Knight left the freshmen in the whole game.
The whole game. And they hustled, and though they
stank at first they got a lot better by the end.

And, surprisingly, wonderfully, so did the starters.
Indiana lost by a school-record score—something
like forty-six points—and at the end of the game it
was the punished, shamed starting players who
rushed off the bench to smack the freshmen on the
tails and buck them up, tell them, No, you guys
played well, never mind the score, man, look at that
shooting percentage in the second half . . . The freshmen perked up. Really? they said. We did okay? You
bet! said the starters, and on and on, right there on
the court. I was sitting three rows away. The Iowa
players couldn't figure it out. They stood off, watching incredulously. Hey—didn't those starters just get
humiliated? And didn't we then beat the sneaks off
the scrubs, by forty-six? What's everybody so happy
about?

Nobody understood. Iowa coach Lute Olson was
furious at Knight, and defended the fact that he ran
up the score (he left *his* starters in until the buzzer;

they were embarrassed every time they made a shot in the last ten minutes) by proclaiming that Knight had "no respect" for the game. Thousands of irate Hoosiers telephoned the athletic director at Indiana and demanded that Knight be fired. Humiliation! Defeat! Knight only made matters worse by telling an interviewer that sometimes winning wasn't as important as other things. "Sometimes," he said, "having to try to win is a nuisance. Winning can really get in the way."

Now *that's* an honest statement that makes sense. And a couple of years later, when Knight won his third national title with some of those freshmen, there was nothing hypocritical or disingenuous about it. Because sometimes winning *isn't* a nuisance, too. Sometimes you have to accept what guys *are*—competitive, scrappy, intense—as you encourage them to be other things they *should*—sensitive, selfless, bighearted. If they're determined to win, well, let them. No one really wants to see them go 7–23 in life.

Arthur Ashe

By the time this appears in print, it is unlikely that Arthur Ashe, who died yesterday at the age of forty-nine, will be getting much ink or airtime. At the moment tributes sing out all over, mostly from people in the worlds of sports and journalism. Ashe's tributes are better than the ones most of our heroes get in the few days after they leave us, even Dizzy Gillespie and Audrey Hepburn, two universally loved idols who also died in recent weeks. You always have to say grandiose things about a public figure who has died, but this time people don't have to rely as much on the somber clichés of admiration and grief. This time the mourning admirers can be honest and spontaneous; they can say what they mean.

This is appropriate, because Ashe always said what he meant. Probably not since Jim Thorpe—except perhaps for the young Muhammad Ali—has there been a champion athlete who never recited one of the standard lines in response to one of the standard questions, who never resorted to the easily uttered expression of easily understood joy, disappointment, determination, sportsmanship, pride, humility, etc., etc., etc. If he found himself with an opportunity to speak when speaking would mean something, Ashe did not waste his chance by using words or ideas others had already worn out.

Why were we able to perceive Ashe's honesty so easily? Because on some intuitive level we recognize that to state frankly a unique, individual feeling requires a unique, individual use of language, and we could not mistake Ashe's discourse for anyone else's. Whether he was analyzing the strategy he used to bamboozle Jimmy Connors in the 1975 Wimbledon final, relating the controversial reasons for visiting South Africa in 1991, or admitting that he had AIDS and fiercely resented being forced to share the "news," Ashe spoke in sentences the form of which seemed to have been invented for the immediate purpose of giving us a startling but unquestionable insight into things.

He said a lot of startling things, but the only thing about him that was ever truly difficult to believe (though you believed it, you believed it) was the magnitude of his intelligence and integrity. Such intelligence is a great gift, enjoyed by very few human beings, even fewer of whom find themselves in the spotlight as often as Ashe did. Especially the spot-

light on a playing field. One had to keep reminding
oneself: "This guy's a *jock*!" It was always revealing
but completely unfair to compare, for example, an
Ashe postgame interview with a similar series of
quotes from anyone else in the world of sports—or,
for that matter, from practically anyone in the world
of politics, or science, or any other field in which we
expect to find bright people. There are some smart
persons out there, and some honest ones, but often
their brains seem to run on gasoline while Ashe's
ran, magically, on white light.

Ashe leaves us with a good lesson: There is a place
in sports for smart people. Intelligence—used well,
in analysis, study, practice—helps you in anything
you try to do, whether it's a backhand lob at a surprising moment or a moral stand on a complex issue.
He was a very talented tennis player, blessed with
extraordinary reach and power and touch, but his
victories were victories of the wits. When he faced
Connors on Centre Court in 1975, it certainly seemed
like old smarts and old bones against the brashly
cruel, indefatigable force and speed of youth. So it
was. Force and speed never had a chance. Ashe
showed that if you are better at thinking, you can
then work hard physically to keep the advantage
when you move into the field of action. Arthur the
Man blew Jimbo the Boy away. Nine years later, Connors gave us the opportunity to see that Ashe's
shrewdness was not just an advantage conferred by
age and experience. In the 1984 final, Jimbo—still

playing in full force as The Boy, despite his senior-
ity—was utterly destroyed by the much smarter John
McEnroe. Like Ashe, McEnroe demonstrated a strategic control (is *that* what manliness is?) that made
Jimmy's reckless force and willful cuteness (and is
that boyishness?) look ridiculous.

It is difficult for an athlete to seem like a man,
rather than like a boy, when we consider him in the
light of the whole world. Sure, as a defensive tackle
is standing there on the sidelines in the fourth quarter after a key goal-line stand, with mud on his face
and sweat running down his bulging neck, brushing
the fatigue off his face with a hand covered in rag-
gedy bandages specked with blood, watching the
game with grim concentration, sure, he seems like
some kind of ultimate paragon of manliness. But off
the playing field, when he's wearing Lycra shorts and
a tank top with REEBOK-EXXON MACHO-NACHO
BOWL, LOS ANGELES 1994 on it as he drives a Jag to
his big intellectual pursuit of watching game films, he
seems rather like a privileged youngster compared
with, say, a Supreme Court justice or a steelworker.
This is not to say athletes (or boys!) are trivial or
superficial people, inherently inferior to the grinds
who toil at graver jobs. We all do what we are best
at doing, especially if it makes us a lot of money,
brings us a lot of satisfaction and prestige, and es-
tablishes us in a position of influence in our social
milieu. We cannot blame sports stars for taking the
obvious path to these felicities. And pro athletes are

not alone in sometimes lacking the manly *gravitas* that compels respect in the broad realm of serious life.

Usually, a successful pro athlete is a man exhibiting the life a boy wants—*as a boy*. But somehow, when a *man* gets there he's supposed to want other things too. He's supposed to know better than to be satisfied with the Jag and the adulation and the triumph during games. Becoming a man means more than living out a fantasy of endless boyhood. The funny thing is, boys know this, even as they fantasize. They know there will be more to it. Listen, boys even know there is more to *boyhood* than the classic carefree life of collecting toads and pulling girls' pigtails. The "more" is the grave imminence of responsible manhood. This is one reason cutesy-boysy jocks like Jimmy Connors seem like such total jerks to boys. It's unnatural for a grown man to try to persist in being The Kid, just as it's unnatural for a ten-year-old boy to try to be The Man. Unfortunately, the rest of us in adult America keep finding such unnaturalness—*both* kinds—just as cute as can be.

Arthur Ashe *emanated* manly *gravitas*. Unlike the football player described above, or the star outfielder who keeps getting arraigned for fighting in bars, or the power forward who spends his time off the court whining about not getting enough respect on it, Ashe never lost his manly quality when the game was over. If anything, he seemed kind of a little bit sillier when he was playing than when he wasn't. Wearing white shorts and holding a racket,

he was great but not at his greatest. How many athletes who achieve the highest championships in their
sport can you say that about? Even when he hoisted
the big silver cups, he never really allowed us to enjoy the illusion other athletes do, which is: This
match is the most important thing in the world right
now. He conveyed the truth that a sport is something a man does part of the time. What he does the
rest of the time, and what he *is*, matters much more,
and it's mostly his own business.

I cannot help thinking about Ashe and Magic
Johnson alongside each other. It is not an irrational
association, nor an unfair one. Both were great
sports champions, great models of a certain kind of
masculine apotheosis, great cultural presences. Also,
of course, both got AIDS. We have just watched Ashe
die of it, and, unfortunately, sometime in the next
few years we will probably watch Magic do the same.
Ashe took his leave with a decisive discretion, in
keeping with his seriousness and the balance he in-
sisted on between public and private responsibility.
Magic's life in public has been much more of an
exuberant party to which we were invited with a grin
and a great wheeling of the arm—*Come on, let's enjoy
me together!* Some have unfairly called Magic a grandstanding show-off—life as one big Pepsi commercial—
but his showing off was incontestably generous: He
was constantly demonstrating what a gas it was to
pay attention to him. If he wasn't particularly serious in any public way before the party got ugly

with plague, we should assume it was because he saw his main responsibility was to share this gift for delight. And even after trying to be a dignified diseased man for a while, Magic gave up and was back knocking on the gym door: Let me in, I can still play. I belong on the Dream Team, because I'm still one of the boys.

To most people, death will seem to be especially cruel when it snatches Magic, crueler than when it took Ashe yesterday. Why? Because even if he lives to be forty-nine, Magic's passing will seem like the death of a child. Don't get me wrong—Magic is a full-grown man and I know it; it would be an error to call him a child just because he grins a lot. But for more complicated reasons, Magic will always seem like a kid to us. Try this test: For a moment forget he is ill, and pretend you have just read that today is Magic Johnson's forty-ninth birthday. Whoa! You are stunned! Magic, almost fifty? No way! It makes you laugh even to consider such a serious number of years trying to lay aholt of Magic. Next thing you know, someone will be telling you Michael Jackson is sixty or something. Ha!

The fact is, the public Magic has never gone beyond the boyish persona that a life in sports defines so readily, so habitually. His glories have all fit into the artificial melodrama that keeps bringing fans to their feet with a roar, in front of bright cameras and eager writers, generation after generation, even to the death. To us, the Magic Man will always be running

with that funny forward-sloping heavy-greyhound pos-
ture, flipping no-look passes to a cutting forward
for a snowbird, smiling with arched eyebrows, winning winning winning—another game, another ring,
then drinking another Pepsi with brimming zest and
a refreshed, forty-four-tooth "Ahhhh!" Brio, energy,
and promise yet to be fully unleashed. It will be Lou
Gehrig all over again—the feeling of a young knight
cut down before he ever got the chance to grow up.
As with Gehrig, America will be incredulous: Is it
even possible that such a guy can die? We will hold
to our disbelief through the inevitable tears, the
swelling tremolo of synth chords accompanying a
slo-mo highlight montage ending in a sweaty Magic
grin frozen in cheer, a purple-and-gold number 32
ascending into the ultimate retirement.

Alas for Ashe, his quiet, seemingly quicker death
strikes us as more natural, less grievous. He was no
boy. In the last few years it has even been difficult
to remember he was an athlete; the somber coach-
teacher role of Davis Cup captain suited his intense
authoritativeness and international sophistication
better. Few of us were really surprised to read that
he was forty-nine. We could have even believed fifty-
five. We did not have to overcome the imagery of
perpetual boyhood in association with Ashe's name
and face: no big smiles, no Pepsi, no insistent playing of his joyous game. I do not mean to cut down
Magic or dismiss him as a lightweight, but as a figure
of a man, he is not in Ashe's league. That's no

criticism, because very, very few people have been in Ashe's league. Somehow, we all knew this—somehow, without a bit of grandstanding, the intelligence and integrity came across.

However, you cannot put intelligence and integrity into a highlight film, or encode them in sentimental lyrics set to obvious music. We cannot recall Arthur Ashe with an image. We look around for his number to retire, and there is no such easy symbol to salute. It is so terribly difficult to remember complicated heroes. Please, guys, can we not forget this one?

Respect

Sitting here sharing a bag of Crazy Chips with Jason LaAntoine Gonzales-Wong, exemplary eleven-year-old male person, and we thought maybe we'd ask him a few last things.

BOOK: Say, JL. Is there one particular single, essential thing that boys need, want, deserve, but do not get from adults? One item?

JL: Oh, sure, man. That's easy.

BOOK: What is it? Patience? Quality time? A bigger allowance? More pizza?

JL: None of that junk. The thing we never get is, respect.

BOOK: Respect?

JL: Yeah. Like, you know, showing the belief that it is even *possible* that sometimes a dude might actually tell the truth, for example, or do something he was asked *nicely* to do instead of hollered at first and demanded? Or maybe not being so sure that you have to rush us along through everything, and take up every minute of our time, because if you give us like two seconds to *think*, then for sure we are going to devise some major awful destructive act. Or not assuming every time that we're going to *fight* you over everything so you have to scare us from the start, so you begin a conversation—*begin* it—by saying like, "Now don't you *dare* even *think* you can get away with blah blah blah."

BOOK: Hmm. I see.

JL: You got any idea how aggressive that is? And how it makes you feel to be so untrusted? "Don't you *dare* . . ." Then, if you even let us tell you something from our side, explain something, you never *believe* us. It's like you're giving us a big break just to even *pretend* to listen but don't.

BOOK: Is this everybody?

JL: Pretty much. It's everybody *we're* supposed to respect, from our side.

Well, JL is right, of course. Boys are supposed to respect adults. But adults definitely do not feel the need to respect boys in return. People may get to know a few boys and allow them to earn some good regard. But respect is a matter of *presuming* goodness from the start, not bestowing a limited trust only after it seems risk-free. Respect is a yes or a no, all or none, a condition upon which everything that follows is built. If there is no respect, nothing is really open to change between people—they just sword fight with finished statements representing finished attitudes.

So how did we come to respect you so little?

A typical adult (yes, there are attitudes typical to adults, more nearly universal than attitudes attributed to gender, race, religious background, etc.) might find it easy to come up with "reasons" for not trusting boys. Boys today, the typical adult says, are violent, contentious, argumentative. They compete in everything and forget the point of the struggle. They jump around, and don't sit and listen. They cuss. They mock. They brag. They shoot each other.

These things are all true. But they are not real reasons. They are excuses, after-the-lack. We come up with them to justify what we automatically felt, even without knowing the latest statistics on middle-school gun offenses or hearing the latest spit-and-cuss lingo. See a boy, feel suspicion. It is what one of my friends calls "a bang-bang thing."

This spontaneous lack of respect *seems* to be profoundly natural. Not even the most self-searching adult is ever bothered by it—no heartfelt looking in the mirror and saying, "I find I don't automatically respect boys. What is *wrong* with me?" Boys, certainly, grow to expect it, after a year or two in school (or earlier, if their parents don't respect them before they even get to school). But there is not a boy in the world who has accepted it without puzzlement, pain, and anger. The boys *do* look in the mirror and say, "Nobody respects me. What is *wrong* with me?" Being suspected of atrocious intentions never comes naturally. Until, finally, you take the hint and begin having atrocious intentions. Then it feels all right.

I don't think the disrespect, for all its profundity, *is* truly a part of nature. But I do think it is so habitual—and so often justified—that it is practically genetically encoded by now. Looking at literature, you can go *way* back—to ancient Greece, if you like, or Vedic India—and still find little treatises on how to control the innate savagery and deceitfulness of young males.

Interestingly, the people who wrote the treatises usually considered themselves advocates *for* boys. In the modern era of Europe and America, this is especially true—the adults who were most outspoken about the bad things that could be expected from boys were the people who tried to create programs for them in which they could thrive despite their inborn savagery. The Boy Scouts, historians tell us, were created so that boys around the turn of the century could (1) express their masculinity and (2) submit to watchful control by adults. At that time,

American society had shifted from agrarian lifestyles to industrial ones; boys, instead of working on their family farms from an early age, were going to school (where they fell under the influence of female teachers) and working in jobs in town. They were being feminized! They needed to rediscover the raw male animal instincts within! But perhaps not *too* raw. We'll start them off exercising their manliness by tying weird knots in string, and then if they do nicely, after that we'll move on to whittling whistles out of pine! What a bunch of masculine fun we'll all have, wearing little uniforms with scarves and badges, and being put to bed early and waked up early and allowed to do absolutely nothing with liberty. Many of the Scouts themselves, of course, were not fooled; they tended to hang around for a year or so, until they could be utterly sure they were being conned, then they dropped out.

The disrespect here is more than a matter of suspicion or distrust. It is a matter of ignoring what the boys themselves might want, because someone else always knows what's best for them. I bet this is what bothered the dropout Boy Scouts in 1906; I know it is what bothers a lot of boys in the 1990s.

Part of the problem has to do with our growing quest for perfection. As our society evolves, we have less and less patience with a healthy mix of strength and flaw in human beings. So many systems around us function with a kind of perfection, whether this means simply the ability to repeat a predictable function over and over again (most machines do this) or to create from simple human input a product that seems inhumanly fine (computer graphics, for example). A half-hour television program could very likely be "imperfect"—in that it could be improved, made more smoothly dramatic by improvements in the editing, say, or funnier through a better use of close-ups at three key moments—but because its appearance is so slick and crisp we do not question it. We do not look for ways in which it could be better largely because we feel no access to the grandiose techniques that produced it. Television seems to embody a perfection all by itself. We cannot help but respect such smoothness; in fact, this is becoming the only kind of thing we *do* respect.

But boys are flagrantly imperfect. Imperfection is what they do best. A boy stands before us as a strange creature, as strange as a computer graphic cartoon of swirling grids going 3-D and turning into a dinosaur and then a spaceship and then the mechanics of photosynthesis at the cellular level. As strange, perhaps, but far less perfect. The boy whines sometimes, sulks sometimes, hits his little brother, breaks things by accident, tells fart jokes, competes, mocks, brags, shoots. So many flaws! We will save our respect until we have something perfect to bestow it on.

But we should resist this effect, especially when it

comes to boys. Can we not treat a boy to the respect we give our democracy? If a candidate gets 55 percent of the vote, he wins the entire election, and even the 45 percent of the people who voted against him go along with the result. In fact, 55–45 is considered a huge victory, a wipeout. But a boy who is 55 percent good is considered a complete loss. He "deserves" almost nothing from us—or at least he *gets* almost nothing.

BOOK: JL—Why do *you* think adults don't respect boys?

JL: You're afraid of us.

BOOK: Oh! Afraid!

JL: Sure. We're gonna shoot you, or mock you, or at least break something made out of glass.

   If JL is right, things are pretty mixed up. Adults, especially men, want boys to respect us but we are afraid of them. Boys want us to respect them, but—with good reason—they fear us too. So everybody is afraid, and nobody is respectful. Are fear and respect so close that they can sub for each other so easily?

   In the Superman comics of my childhood there was a wonderful antagonist the Man of Steel kept coming up against, a creature named Bizarro. Bizarro looked quite a bit like Superman himself, but everything was a little off center and off-color, from his body to his feelings to his uniform. Bizarro had been created when Superman was shot by a faulty ray gun that was supposed to make duplicates of things but instead produced weird variations, crude mockeries of the original. Bizarro had superpowers, just like the Supe, but he was wild and suspicious and could turn ugly. Often, when confronting him, Superman had to look into himself to see where one of Bizarro's traits came from; then he could figure out how it could be stopped.

Well, it seems to me that fear is the Bizarro of respect. It's a crude mockery of respect in its own image. They both involve a certain awe, but where fear is superficial and twists things around, respect is profound and stable. The difference is not that hard to figure out: What creates respect is understanding.

Boys and men have to recognize that we want the same things from each other. This is natural, because we are not all that different. A man is still living much of a boy's life, though he loses sight of this as he grows. And a boy, as we have seen, is living much of a man's life in advance. They cannot be each other, but they can recognize each other. If a man seems to be a boy hit with a faulty ray gun, or a boy seems that way to a man, it may be because they are ignoring what they know, what they truly understand. Men are trying hard to inspire in boys the traits they want to respect in themselves. Boys are trying hard to grow in those same ways. The best way to make boys respectful is to be that way ourselves. That's the best way to make them honest, generous, tough, funny, and wise too.

Let's face it: Boys will always be what men will always be.

About the Author

Bruce Brooks, author of the Newbery Honor Books *The Moves Make the Man* and *What Hearts,* as well as other award-winning titles, appears regularly in schools around the country. He and his wife live in Silver Spring, Maryland, where they are raising their two sons.